# THE
# SOOTERKIN

VIKING

*75 years*

BY THE SAME AUTHOR

*Trial and Error: Mordechai Vanunu and Israel's Nuclear Bomb*
(with John McKnight)

# THE
# SOOTERKIN

## TOM GILLING

VIKING

VIKING
Published by the Penguin Group
Penguin Putnam Inc., 375 Hudson Street,
New York, New York 10014, U.S.A.
Penguin Books Ltd, 27 Wrights Lane, London W8 5TZ, England
Penguin Books Australia Ltd, Ringwood, Victoria, Australia
Penguin Books Canada Ltd, 10 Alcorn Avenue,
Toronto, Ontario, Canada M4V 3B2
Penguin Books (N.Z.) Ltd, 182–190 Wairau Road,
Auckland 10, New Zealand

Penguin Books Ltd, Registered Offices:
Harmondsworth, Middlesex, England

First American edition
Published in 2000 by Viking Penguin,
a member of Penguin Putnam Inc.

1 3 5 7 9 10 8 6 4 2

AUTHOR'S NOTE
Some incidents and characters' names have been drawn from
the columns of early colonial newspapers. Dennis Todd's book
*Imagining Monsters* (1995) was a valuable source of information
on sooterkins and other curious births, while Johann Caspar
Lavater's *Essays on Physiognomy* (1798) taught me the finer points
of that abstruse science.

CIP data available.

ISBN 0-670-89152-5

This book is printed on acid-free paper.

Printed in the United States of America
Set in Baskerville MT

*For Rosemary, Mum and Dad*

# THE
# SOOTERKIN

PARDON THE stench. You have hardly turned a page and a blast of putrid air has pricked your nostrils. The smell of mud and smoke and sickness, of spoiled meat and mouldy straw and slops left to rot in the street. Had you come sooner, you would have smelt eucalyptus blossom and lavender and Kentish hops struggling up the trellis in the chaplain's garden.

It is May 1812 and winter is almost here. The whales have come early and Hobart Town is rancid with blubber. The try-pots have been boiling for a week and won't be doused until the last whale has been barrelled. The wharves are slippery with spilt oil. There is blood in the streets and piles of guts washed up on the beach.

And mud. Dark, stinking mud churned up by cartwheels and flung by horses' hooves until the walls and windows of every house are spattered with it.

In short, there are better times to visit this island and you would be well advised to catch the next schooner to Sydney, if there is room on it. You will find the office in

Macquarie Street, the blue-painted door near the bond store: James McCluskey, Ships' Agent. McCluskey is the gentleman in the armchair, white-haired with a lazy eye and whiskers clotted with bacon fat. That eye is the most energetic thing about him. The rest hardly stirs between breakfast and supper. But McCluskey will get you a berth, if there are berths to be got.

In the meantime, a few drops of lavender water sprinkled on a handkerchief will make the air more bearable. Ellis in Argyle Street has bottles in the window which he may be persuaded to sell for half a crown.

~

ON THIS dull, windy afternoon a spidery figure in corduroy trousers and leather waistcoat is weaving his way up Argyle Street with a parcel of oysters under his arm. There is something verminous about him, a suggestion of infestation emphasised by his habit of stopping abruptly in the middle of the road and scratching his head.

The man is William Dyer, forty-six years old, a thin-necked, sallow-cheeked veteran of the Peninsular Wars. Twice promoted corporal, twice reduced to the ranks. Served at Corunna, Talavera, Busaco, Badajoz, Albuera. Wounded five times, viz Corunna, Talavera, Busaco, Badajoz, Albuera. William Dyer never entered a battle without being stretchered off it. He was twice taken with typhoid fever, three times with the pox. Dishonourably discharged Cadiz, Spain. Pay owing: ninepence. Arrived Hobart Town, Van Diemen's Land, November 1811. Married Sarah Moody, twenty-four, convict, fair complexion, blue eyes, three months pregnant. There is not much of William Dyer that has not been whittled away by typhoid and thin rations. The flesh that was on him once has fallen off, leaving a lean, sparrow-boned handsomeness that makes him look ten years younger than he is.

Dyer's slovenly gait mimics the undulations of the road as it rises from the yellow cliff above Sullivan's Cove before lurching down to the rivulet and then resuming its climb towards the wooded hills overlooking the harbour.

Of all the streets in Hobart Town, Argyle Street is the most rebellious. While other streets obey the judicious symmetry of Governor Macquarie's grid, Argyle flouts it with a maze of squalid alleys and gangways leading down to a wooded gorge much favoured by escaping convicts. Spurning the brick houses and public monuments of its neighbours, Argyle Street revels in its surly collection of weatherboard shacks and taverns and narrow-fronted shops fencing stolen goods.

At the point where the road ends among a rabble of settlers' huts and rickety boarding houses, William Dyer pauses to hitch up his trousers. A work gang shuffles past on its way to the lumber yard: six men in coarse canary jackets and caps, stiff leather slippers, rusty chains sagging from their belts, staring at the parcel under his arm.

A half-starved dog limps out to meet him. Dyer looks around, as if its appearance signals a more dangerous welcome lying just out of sight. He walks back a few yards to peer down an alley, then crosses the street, glances over his shoulder and clumsily reties the string holding his trousers up. Having satisfied himself that the dog's companions are elsewhere, he picks up a stone and hurls it, losing his balance and falling down in the mud at exactly the moment that Sarah Dyer gives birth to his son.

~

'WHAT'S THIS?' growls Dyer, as if someone has played a trick while his back was turned. He stares at the boy, curled up like a prawn on an oily sheepskin, pink and wrinkly, shit-smeared, eyes pinched against the candlelight. 'I thought it weren't due for a fortnight.' His breath reeks of beer and tobacco. A mudcake is stuck to his backside. 'God bless him, missus, but the boy's got a decent bit of gear on him.'

The midwife has just got him tied off and is soaping her hands in a basin.

Dyer pokes a tar-stained finger between the child's gums, then counts his toes and pinches his ribs and slaps his shrivelled bum. 'What's his name then?'

'He hasn't got one,' says Sarah Dyer, sitting up in bed so she can keep watch on the pair of them. She is a quick-tempered woman with a small red mouth and too many teeth. Something about her lips suggests a pout that has fallen out of use. It was never her intention to shackle herself to an insipid creature like William Dyer, but there is only so much of a man's character that can be discerned while rutting in the dark against a ship's bulkhead.

Dyer wipes the goo off his finger and peers into the boy's ears, which are already settling into a familiar spiral shape, like cabbage hearts, the spitting image of his own. 'William ain't a bad name,' he says.

'Suit yourself,' says Sarah, lowering herself back on her pillow. She glances sideways at the midwife, whose face is fixed in a solemn grimace of disapproval. 'I've got nothing against William.'

Dyer rubs his chin and says, 'Thomas is a good'n.' He leans over and picks a stray bit of sheep's wool out of the child's ear. 'A boy'd go a long way with Thomas behind him...or Joshua.'

'He only needs the one,' she says. 'Which is it to be?'

Dyer pushes his clay pipe between his lips and sucks on the empty bowl. 'Ned,' he says. 'I never seen a boy go wrong with Ned.'

'Ned it is then.'

Dyer flips the boy over and starts tickling him with his pipe stem. As he draws curlicues on the child's belly, a blob of black tar rolls out and comes to rest in his navel. The midwife stops what she's doing and puffs up like a pigeon. If there was a broomstick in her hand, she would clout him with it.

She frowns at the child and sets to work with soap and bacon fat and witch-hazel while William Dyer stands shame-faced in the corner nursing his oysters. But the blob refuses to move, and the midwife says it's stuck fast and will have to be burnt out with a candle or sucked out with a poultice or left where it is.

'A bit of tar never did a boy any harm,' mumbles Dyer.

'And what would you know about it?' snaps his wife.

The midwife goes home and Sarah Dyer falls asleep and her husband beavers away with a saucer of sour milk and a sponge and some lavender water he found in a bottle by the road. But nothing will shift the blob and after an hour of rubbing and cursing he gives up and goes back to his oysters.

~

WE HAVE skipped ahead nine years to a grey wet winter of fog and squalls. The River Derwent has burst its banks and sheep are drowning from Jericho to Clarence Plains. Trading ships lie at anchor in Sullivan's Cove, creaking, taking on water above and below. Last week a squid was found swimming in the harbourmaster's basement.

Lieutenant-Governor Davey, caught with his hands in the regimental pay chest, has been removed from his post and banished with a hundred head of cattle to his farm in Pitt Water. His replacement, Colonel Sorell, an honest fornicator, petitions London for more soldiers to keep the blacks at bay and guard his five thousand convicts. There is fever in the gaol. The causeway to Hunter's Island has been washed away and rebuilt and washed away again, so that condemned men must wade ashore to be hanged.

Ned has grown into a dark-haired, sinewy lad dressed in his father's corduroy pants cut off at the knee, with a calico shirt and blood-red double-tied neckerchief. He can fillet a gentleman's pockets with a shaving razor and separate a widow from her silk handkerchief. He can tell a tin watch from a silver one, spot if a coin has been clipped and judge an ounce of tobacco by looking at it. Such talents are not to be despised in a boy who has the wit to put them to use. But they don't impress Mrs Fitzgerald, the schoolmistress.

Mrs Fitzgerald is a bustling, wattle-throated woman who arrived in the colony seeking eligible bachelors but, finding none to her taste, assumed a vocation that made them unnecessary. The existence, now or in the past, of a Mr

Fitzgerald is a question much speculated on by Hobart
society, but never resolved.

It is Mrs Fitzgerald's philosophy that children—and
especially boys—must have education forced into them, as
a French farmer forces grain down a goose's gullet. A boy,
she says, who cannot acquaint himself with the contents
of a newspaper or read his name on a summons is a boy
who will never know which side of the world is up.

Ned, having swallowed his lessons for the time it took
to learn his letters, add ninepence halfpenny to half a crown
and divide a pound of almonds by four, is convinced that
the rest can be acquired by practice. Every morning he
spends an hour wandering the streets, poring over signs
and notices, mouthing words in shop windows, reading
aloud from papers trodden into the mud.

On the corner of Collins and Elizabeth streets, opposite the shop of Messrs Lloyd and Lonsdale, suppliers of
gentlemen's and ladies' garments, English and India
chintzes, calicoes, slops and flannel, stands a dead gum tree,
rust-streaked from the nails hammered into it.

The smooth grey trunk is used as a noticeboard for the
display of government proclamations and private adver-
tisements that would otherwise have to be paid for in the
columns of the *Hobart Town Gazette*. Rewards are posted on
it; inventories of stolen property; lost and found notices;
threats of litigation and offers of land for quick sale; warnings against trespassers and appeals for the return of stray
bullocks. Sometimes a copy of the *Gazette* is hung up in the
hope of attracting subscribers.

The tree is a signpost to what the colony is doing, what
it's thinking, what it fears and what it admires, what it will

pay and what it won't. It is here that Ned offers his services, at a halfpenny a time, to the convict servants and rheumy-eyed ticket-of-leave men who can't read for themselves.

Amid the reports of animals lost, crops rotted and furniture floating out to sea, Ned fastens on a small item in the newspaper:

> Born to Mr Galloway's grey Mare: a two-legged Colt. The pitiful Creature is in all Respects perfect save for the want of its Forelegs.

Ned is curious to see the creature, although he can't be sure from the newspaper's description whether the colt has two legs, four legs or no legs. If it were not for the floods, he would walk out to Galloway's farm and count them for himself.

Meanwhile Sarah Dyer is bulging again, to the consternation of Ned (who will have to share a bed) and the surprise of his father (who cannot recall playing any part in it).

The midwife who delivered Ned is long dead from cholera, buried in the graveyard behind the barracks with her daughter beside her. Now the maternity trade belongs to Mrs Jakes, the chaplain's housekeeper, who caters to all except the gentry. They would rather have Mr Trelawny because he comes to the door in a dog cart and carries a leather bag, while Mrs Jakes walks and carries a canvas sack.

Trelawny is a bleeder by choice but will try his hand at anything when the grog is on him. Hobart Town is full of officers who owe their ruptures to Trelawny, and lunatics who owe him their trepannings. There is many a gentleman's son carrying Trelawny's purple thumbprints on his skull, and many a baby with his bones snapped by the forceps and his mother opened up like a purse, so Trelawny could reach in and pluck out his guinea before the father got home.

Ned and his mother are swinging a bucket of mussels when Trelawny catches sight of them in Argyle Street. 'I'll consent to deliver the child for half a guinea,' he says, slowing his beast to a trot.

'Not from me you won't,' says Sarah Dyer.

'I shan't require the money at once,' says Trelawny, clip-clopping through the puddles.

She hisses at Ned to take no notice.

'I've seen a hundred mothers die that were too stubborn to let a doctor lay a hand on them.'

'Mussels thruppence a bag.'

'Don't imagine, ma'am, that I am in need of patients, or that the fee is of any material importance, or that I approach you with anything but the strongest feelings of disinterest.'

'I never imagined nothing,' says Sarah.

'I dare say, ma'am, in light of your circumstances'—he glances at the bucket—'I might be persuaded to reduce my fee to something more appropriate to your means. I may be induced to accept five shillings.'

'Mrs Jakes will deliver me cheap enough.'

'Indeed, ma'am,' says Trelawny, 'Mrs Jakes will deliver you to your maker if you are not careful. There is as much medicine in that woman as there is in my horse.'

Sarah Dyer stops where she is and puts the bucket down and gives the animal such a whack on the rump that it bolts down the hill, with Trelawny tangled up in the reins and a pack of barking dogs strung out behind him like seagulls after a whaler.

Ned glances at his mother's belly. 'Are you going to die, Mam?'

'Does it look like it?' she says.

The boy doesn't know. The pair of them stop to watch the pot-bellied figure of the Reverend Mr Kidney emerging blearily from Mr Birch's grand house in Macquarie Street. Conscious of being stared at, the chaplain pauses beside a rhododendron bush and buries his nose in a large white handkerchief, where he remains honking and snorting until Mr Goldfarb crosses the road to see if he is dying. Mr Kidney explains that he is not, but thanks him for his concern.

A week before the baby is due, the midwife paddles through the gate. A stout, square-jawed woman with a cotton mob-cap screwed down tight on a bun of steel-grey hair, Mrs Jakes approaches her profession with the same serenity she would bring to stuffing a marrow, or wringing the neck of a chicken.

She allows no room for sentimentality. Her detachment is such as to have persuaded some mothers, gratefully delivered of a healthy child, that Mrs Jakes once knew that joy and had it wrenched from her. Some have confided their thoughts to Mrs Jakes and been chastised for it, and told to mind their own business, which has only made their suspicions deeper.

Mrs Jakes doesn't send Ned out of the house but kneels down and puts her hands on Sarah Dyer's belly. She asks when the baby is due, then reaches under the mother's skirts. Her eyebrows show a flicker of surprise.

'I hope there is nothing unusual,' says Sarah. She smiles over her shoulder at Ned, whose gaze is fixed on a large mole growing on Mrs Jakes's chin, with hairs sprouting from it like the bristles on an artist's brush.

The midwife removes her hand but doesn't answer. She asks if there is brandy in the house, should the occasion demand it. She declines the offer of a biscuit.

~

THE REVEREND Mr Kidney is a short round bowlegged man with black muttonchop whiskers and a florid face, like a pomegranate, into which he has poured a great quantity of brandy and lesser amounts of whisky and claret.

Mr Kidney prefers to drink in company, but when there is none to be had he is willing—more than willing—to drink alone. He knows when to stop, but in an abstract, impersonal way, the way he knows the Latin name for a cucumber and the number of chapters in Ezekiel.

He wears a straight-cut, single-breasted coat with an upright collar and sleeves which stop several inches short of his wrists—the same coat he wore when he came ashore on a blustery afternoon in 1804, except that the mother-of-pearl buttons have been replaced with bone and the seams have been let out more than once.

Mr Kidney came as chaplain to the colony of Van Diemen's Land at a salary—less generous than he had been promised—of one hundred and eighty-two pounds and ten shillings per annum.

In the inside pocket of his coat was a letter from his brother-in-law, a lawyer with an estate on the banks of the

Hawkesbury River, thirty miles from Sydney. The letter, written in a hand he did not immediately recognise, extolled the benevolent climate, the green hills and fertile valleys, the rich dark soil and rivers teeming with fish and suggested, somewhat condescendingly, that a humble clergyman (which Mr Kidney was not) might do worse than set himself up in the new colony of Van Diemen's Land, where it was said a fortune could be made with very little effort.

The idea of a fortune made without effort (he was not an attentive reader) appealed to Mr Kidney, as did the distance that would suddenly open up between himself and a small but awkward circle of creditors. The sums concerned were modest, even trifling, but the demands for their repayment were becoming peremptory. He was careful not to broadcast his intention of leaving.

He knew scarcely anything about Van Diemen's Land, and not much more about his brother-in-law, except that he owned land in New South Wales equivalent to a sizeable chunk of Oxfordshire and had paid next to nothing for it. What he did know was that the colony had a vacancy for a chaplain; and this fact, together with the contents of his brother-in-law's letter, was enough to make up his mind.

Mr Kidney discovered too late that his brother-in-law had never been south of Botany Bay. His knowledge of Van Diemen's Land came from a Scottish sealer who traded in Maori heads. The sealer had heard about it from the captain of a Boston whaler who had once ridden out a storm in Norfolk Bay. The Boston sea captain got it from the surgeon on a convict ship. The surgeon was a drunkard and made it up.

Mr Kidney found himself in a shanty town, a jumble of tents and timber huts. Sawn logs and casks of nails and pickled herrings were stacked haphazardly by the shore. Convicts huddled under tarpaulins and the stench of smoke and boiling blubber drifted from the whalers' try-pots in Storm Bay.

The hills beyond the settlement were strangled with thick forests. Sheep sank up to their necks in swamps. Rivers ran brown from the tannin in the button grass. The body of an absconder was found, half-eaten by wild animals, with sharpened sticks poking out of his eye sockets.

For a year Mr Kidney lived in a tent. Convicts broke into his trunk and stole his clothes, his books, his china. He was plagued by boils and blowflies. He suffered delirious fevers and biblical constipations. But for Lord Spencer's brandy, it is doubtful he would have survived the winter.

But he did survive, when others didn't, and he thanked God and Lord Spencer for preserving him. He supervised the construction of a stone cottage with a garden and a cellar and a small jetty where he could sit on warm days and fish for mackerel. As chaplain he refused to settle for fewer than six shuttered windows, of which three must be facing north. He didn't mind that the floors were not level and the doors were not square, so long as the roof didn't leak.

Mr Kidney had convicts dig flowerbeds and drainage channels and build retaining walls. He acquired a broad-brimmed hat to protect himself from the sun, with a muslin gauze to keep off the flies. He strode about the garden ordering the removal of eucalypts and she-oaks and their replacement with marrows and cabbages and runner beans.

He wrote to the Bishop of Calcutta asking for cuttings. The bishop sent him oranges, lemons, limes, neatly packed in sandalwood boxes, but already withered from the sea air. And a portable pulpit, made of teak, which he had not asked for and would have used for firewood had his housekeeper, Mrs Jakes, not found it useful for storing umbrellas.

Later gifts (apples, gooseberries, quinces) were more successful, flourishing in the dark soil. Mr Kidney came to see their fecundity as a symbol of his own endeavour, ignoring the convict gardeners who, over the years, wore themselves out clearing rocks and shovelling shit on his beds. He sensed that God was pleased with him, and that he deserved it. He drank to his success and was disinclined to stop.

~

A Cucumber of large Size was grown this Season on a natural Bed in the Garden of the Rev. Mr Kidney at Cottage Green; its Length was $14\frac{1}{2}$ inches; Girth 12 ditto; Weight 4 lbs. We are pleased to congratulate Mr Kidney on its Production.

~

AT A minute before three on Saturday afternoon, the 14th of July, 1821, Sarah Dyer feels an impatient kick.

It is a dismal, squally day with sleet scratching the rooftops and smoke curling over the town like a rat's tail. William Dyer, two-thirds drunk after his morning's

*14*

exertions on the wharves, is trying to stitch up the holes in his lobster pot. Ned is making hooks out of sewing needles. Sarah is sitting down, legs apart, elbows on her knees, staring at a plate of bread and dripping.

Suddenly she cries out, 'God save me! It's happening.' She tries to stand up. A gallon of murky water spills out of her. She groans and clutches her belly. William Dyer turns as pale as tripe.

Before Ned can open the door, the midwife shuffles in, all pink forearms and broad hips and bunions, with a canvas sack as big as a goat slung over her shoulder. She pays no attention to the shrieking mother-to-be but fastens her gaze on the others as she pushes her grey hair under the flaps of her mob-cap and ties the strings firmly under her chin.

Then it's hot water and towels and the midwife on her hands and knees and Sarah Dyer thrashing like a calf being dragged to the butcher's yard and Ned huddled under the table watching it all through the slits in his fingers.

He hears cries, shouts, his mother squealing at the pain, William Dyer grinding his teeth on the stem of his pipe, the midwife up to her elbows in blood and pig's grease and God knows what else she has in her bag of tricks.

Finally out it comes, a thing the size of a weasel, wet and slippery and covered in fur. The boy feels a hard lump drop down his throat into the pit of his stomach. His mouth opens and shuts and a warm wetness leaks out of him, soaking the legs of his trousers. For a moment he feels the breath sucked right out of his lungs.

'A boy!' shouts Dyer, although the creature has got flippers and a black snout and resembles no boy that was ever born.

'Mercy!' cries Sarah Dyer, falling back on her pillows.

If Mrs Jakes has any opinion on the subject, she keeps it to herself. She picks the thing up and stares at it impassively, as if she were guessing the meat on a rabbit. The faintest shadow of a smile passes over her face, imperceptible to anyone except Sarah Dyer, who is watching her out of one eye. Mrs Jakes glances at Ned, still hiding under the table, with a puddle spreading under his feet, and says, 'It'll want a name, whatever it is.'

~

During the Day and Night of Thursday, and all day Friday, rough Weather with incessant Rain prevailed. The Torrent of Water which has flowed down the Rivulet has done considerable Harm. The Banks in some Places have been undermined and loosened, and some Houses have been damaged; and we lament to say that the new Brick Bridge in Murray-street, which was nearly completed, and would have been passable early next Week, was torn down.

~

THE REVEREND Mr Kidney stands under his black umbrella, staring at the rubble of Captain Nairn's brick bridge. Exactly a week ago the building superintendent, Mr Farquhar, stood on the dais, scratching his arse with a bevel square, and pronounced it the sturdiest bridge in the colony.

The dais is still standing: a stout wooden frame with a

carved balustrade and an ingenious set of wheels, built to the carpenter's own design, which give it the appearance of a medieval siege engine. But the bridge is in ruins, its humble arch swept away in the torrent, and with it the reputations of Mr Farquhar and Captain Nairn. And the chaplain, instead of leading the colony in prayer, has been laid up in bed with the flu, fending off Trelawny's leeches.

It is Saturday afternoon and the settlement seems strangely deserted, as if its citizens had had enough of the mud and taken refuge in the hills. Sheepishly Mr Kidney climbs the steps of the dais. It's a relief to him that the bridge was destroyed before he blessed it, rather than after. He is grateful to the Lord for sparing him that little humiliation. His reputation at the moment, owing to some unkind rumours about his health, and his difficulty in honouring certain debts, is not at such a high point that it would easily shake off such a malicious demonstration of his impotence.

Mr Kidney lays his fat pink hands on the wooden rail and stares disconsolately at the rubble. There are footprints all over the bank. Further off he notices the deep ruts of a bullock cart. And a wheelbarrow, turned upside-down to ensure it doesn't sail away in the deluge. And a set of pulley ropes still hanging from the dais on which the lieutenant-governor was to have sat while he, Thomas Kidney, led them in prayer. An illicit army, better organised than the one that built the bridge, and more enterprising, has been carting off the bricks. In a day or two there will be nothing left but the sandstone footings.

The chaplain feels a sharp pain somewhere inside the damp cocoon of his coat; a pang not unconnected with an overlarge breakfast of devilled kidneys but sharpened by disappointment and a growing conviction that life has not honoured the promises it made to him. His hopes (surely not extravagant) were for a civilised, prosperous society respectful of God and the law. He did not expect literature and cathedrals. But even those modest dreams now seem as flimsy as Captain Nairn's brick bridge.

He fishes in his coat for the silver flask which is all that keeps him from being sucked dry by Trelawny's leeches. If leeches ever acquired a taste for brandy, instead of dropping off half-full with their tails shaking, Mr Kidney would not be confident of surviving his next bout of flu. He swallows a mouthful, holds the flask to his chest, then swallows another. His left hand grips the rail, which sways under his weight. He notices several banisters are missing. He backs away until he is standing in the middle of the dais, a condemned man waiting to fall through a trap door—into what?

Glancing behind him at a line of scraggy poplars planted beside the mill race, the chaplain sees a dark stooping figure scratching, like a chicken, among the undergrowth. The black shovel hat conceals the bald speckled head of James Sculley, a short wiry widower of sixty-four winters who arrived in the colony in 1813 and lives on an income of five hundred pounds sterling per annum, paid quarterly by a firm of solicitors in Southampton.

When not rummaging under bushes, Mr Sculley can often be seen skulking in the woods or prowling along the shore. He collects and catalogues unusual specimens, draws meticulous sketches of birds, reptiles and mammals that have expired in his gas jar, then dissects them and reassembles their skeletons (discarding the pieces that won't fit) on copper wire. Such habits, in the chaplain's eyes, constitute evidence of a macabre and unhealthy enthusiasm for science.

The beach below Battery Point is Mr Sculley's favourite hunting-ground, a great sieve that catches every kind of flotsam: the bodies of stranded dolphins and drowned sailors; planks of English oak, shards of porcelain and rough egg-shaped cinders skimmed off whalers' try-pots; jellyfish and broken bottles and the carcass of a mule that trotted into the sea and swam out until it was exhausted and was brought back by the tide, its teeth picked clean by sea lice and crabs scuttling in its ears.

According to the latest rumours, he is now immersed in the science of physiognomy, the divining of a person's character by the shape of their features, and is preparing a paper on the subject for the inaugural meeting of the Van Diemen's Land Scientific Society.

The chaplain watches as Mr Sculley unearths something from among the dead leaves and deposits it furtively in the pocket of his black frockcoat. He is tempted to call out, merely for the sake of letting him know that he is being observed. But as this might suggest some curiosity on his part he decides against it and reverses down the steps.

When Mr Kidney reaches the bottom he is startled to find a white-haired old man sheltering under the dais. Beside him is a small handcart stacked with bricks. The man is sitting on a large timber block, with his back to him, smoking a pipe.

Taking note of his age and probable infirmity, the chaplain decides to confront him, to berate him for stealing the government's bricks. But the man hardly appears capable of filling the cart, let alone absconding with it. What looks like his left arm, hanging limply by his side, is on closer inspection an empty sleeve.

Ahurrgh. Mr Kidney clears his throat.

The old man ignores him and carries on puffing his pipe.

'You, sir.'

The man raises one cheek and farts boisterously.

'I am addressing you, sir.'

He gazes carelessly behind him and suddenly sees the chaplain there, less than an arm's length away. 'Beg pardon, sir, I never heard yur honour.' He hastily stuffs the pipe in his pocket. 'I'm mostly deaf, sir…too much wax in the ears…I have to see the words comin' out, sir, else I can't make sense of 'em.'

Mr Kidney gives the old man a look which says he does not believe him but is prepared (he hoists his black umbrella) to give him the benefit of the doubt. He looks again at the handcart. 'You intend to steal these bricks?'

'Steal 'em? No, sir, not a bit of it.' The invalid holds up his empty sleeve. 'I'm keepin' an eye on 'em, sir.' He nods gravely. 'Makin' sure no-one runs off with 'em.'

The chaplain is momentarily nonplussed. A pathetic gratitude surges through him. His umbrella trembles with the discovery that common English honesty has not been entirely washed away in the deluge. 'For Mr Farquhar?'

'Farker, sir?'

'The building superintendent.'

The old man shakes his head. 'For Mrs Sweetwater, sir.'

Mr Kidney blinks. He gulps. A look comes over him that suggests the onset of sudden paralysis. 'Mrs Sweetwater?'

'What?'

'You mentioned Mrs Sweetwater.'

The man pushes his index finger into his ear with every intention, it seems, of locating the obstruction and pushing it out the other side. 'Sweetwater, sir. 'Er of the 'orticultural society. She wants 'em for 'er greenhouse. Give me thruppence to keep 'em safe.'

Mr Kidney stares at the bricks, as though expecting them to rise up from the handcart and form themselves into some angular likeness of the lady whose friendship he once enjoyed, but whose attentions he has lately felt compelled to curb. He never ventured far enough into Mrs Sweetwater's feelings to discover the precise nature of her affections, nor far enough into his own to ascertain whether or how much they might be reciprocated. Mrs Jakes did not hide her disapproval and the chaplain, unwilling to question her motives, allowed himself to be swayed. The thought that Mrs Sweetwater might now be implicated in some activity involving bricks is something Mr Kidney cannot bring himself to contemplate. He looks at the man, who is still attempting to dislodge something from his ear, and effects a muddled escape under the cover of his umbrella.

~

A TEARFUL wail bursts from Sarah Dyer—a wail so long and so loud as to staunch the flow from Ned's bladder and bring a deep frown to the face of Mrs Jakes.

'Get a hold, missus,' says William Dyer, not wanting to peer too closely at the thing his wife has brought into the world.

They all stare at Ned, as if they are expecting him to jump up and hug the creature.

Suddenly they notice a face squinting at them through the window. A thin, hatchet face with sharp yellow teeth and eyes scrunched up like oysters.

William Dyer staggers to his feet but immediately falls down again. The intruder stays there, his nose pressed flat to the glass. Then, in an instant, he's gone.

Sarah Dyer, quickly regaining her composure, glances at her husband and snaps, 'Go after him, boy. Find out his business.'

Ned scrambles out just in time to see the emaciated figure slither round the corner into Murray Street. He hobbles down the hill, slipping and sliding in the mud, his torn brown jacket hanging off his shoulders like a potato sack. His right leg has a mind of its own, jerking out from under him as if someone was pulling it with a string. The gait of a convict, or one who used to be—a ticket-of-leave man let out for good behaviour before his seven years was up. Hobart Town is full of them, spastic puppets dragging around imaginary leg irons, hungrier than the dogs that lope after them.

He pushes past an old woman selling faggots, splashing through the mud, dragging his crazy foot after him. Ned backs into a doorway as the man skids to a halt outside the police magistrate's house, a square, red-brick house with heavy stone lintels over the doors and windows and a steep slate roof. There is a small brass plaque on the gatepost with the inscription 'A.W.H. Humphrey, Chief Magistrate of Police'. Grey-brown smoke is leaking from the chimney—a miserly fire kept alive with green timber. A pair of wolfhounds are stretched out on long chains, indifferent to the rain, or preferring it to whatever is indoors.

The ticket-of-leave man pulls a rag out of his trousers and spits on it, then looks over his shoulder and starts rubbing the grime off his face. Or rather, wiping it off one cheek and wiping it back on the other. He spits on his hands and stamps the mud off his boots and slicks his greasy black hair over his skull. Then he stuffs the rag back in his pocket, hitches up his trousers and rings the bell.

~

Mr SCULLEY, of Elizabeth-street, will be glad to host the inaugural Meeting of the Van Diemen's Land Scientific Society, on Saturday evening, where several INTERESTING MATTERS will be discussed. Ladies welcome.

~

'I SAW it, sir. God knows I wish I never had but I saw it slither out of her with my own eyes.' The man pulls at the baggy skin under his eyes, so that his bloodshot eyeballs seem ready to roll out of their sockets. 'God strike me down if I didn't.'

'He will strike you down,' says Mrs Humphrey. 'You may count on it.' She removes the scented handkerchief from her nose, revealing a pale, fine-boned and still youthful face set off with a black velvet choker from which her husband's miniature only briefly hung.

'The fool's been drinking,' says Mr Humphrey, his own large, ruddy face suggestive of anything but the unmitigated pleasure of his wife's company. 'I can smell it on him.'

Mrs Humphrey leans forwards in her chair and says, with ominous precision, 'You know Mr Humphrey deplores liars.'

'Tain't a lie, missus. Tis God's own naked truth.'

'I refuse to listen to this,' snaps Humphrey. He looks balefully at the ticket-of-leave man and mouths some indistinct threat before snatching up his spectacles and walking out.

Mrs Humphrey rests her left hand on the arm of the chair and takes in the finer details of the man's appearance. There is dried blood around his left eye and clods of mud stuck to the shells of his ears. A gap between his crooked front teeth holds the remnants of recent meals, deposited layer by layer, like soil strata. His trouser legs are unravelling, exposing a pair of thin scabby ankles.

She clutches the handkerchief to her nose and requests him to stand further off, near the open window. 'Now tell me again,' she says. 'Exactly as before. Leave nothing out.'

'Like I said, missus, I had me face stuck to the glass, starin' inside, when I seen this thing come out of her, brown and shiny like an eel, and her squealing like someone cut her belly open with a knife and blood everywhere and the fat one trying to catch hold of it and slippin' and splashin' in the waters and flippers on it and no arms and God knows what it was horrible only it came out of her just like it was one of her own flesh and blood and I says to myself: go and tell Mr Humphrey, if it's a monster he's got to hear of it and pull the law down on its head.'

Mrs Humphrey nods slowly. The colony seems prone to unnatural couplings and grotesque deformities in its livestock, but this is the first account of human monstrosity to have reached her ears. 'And what advantage did you expect to gain by this information?'

'Advantage, missus?'

'What profit did you hope to make from your story?'

The convict screws up his face so hard that four black stripes appear across his forehead. 'No profit, missus.'

'You were not anticipating a reward?'

He shifts his weight from one spindly leg to the other. 'No, missus, only...'

'Only what?'

'A shilling'd be handsome.'

'A shilling!'

'A tanner then, missus.' He sniffs and wipes his nose on his sleeve. 'For the wife.'

Mrs Humphrey's gaze drops to the novel resting in her lap, whose protagonist (a short, malicious man with a fastidious taste in riding boots) bears an uncanny likeness to her husband. She slips a black ribbon between its pages. 'There is no risk of this—tanner—being used for anything else?'

He grips his right leg to stop it twitching. 'No, missus.'

Mrs Humphrey looks at him, as if to say that of all the sixpences now circulating in Hobart Town this particular coin will not change hands without her hearing of it, and that any attempt to divert it from its stated purpose will be severely dealt with. She judges by the rush of blood to his face that the gist of her meaning has penetrated the mud stoppers in his ears, then drops the coin into his palm and rings for a servant to remove him.

~

EMERGING FROM the poplar trees with his prize (the body of a small mouse, slightly decomposed), Mr Sculley is at once exposed to the inquisitorial gaze of a donkey and its owner, a timbercutter, who jointly arrive at the conclusion that he is a sinister apparition and not to be approached.

They flinch at the sight of his frockcoat, a long black garment, iridescent from wear, that falls almost to his ankles and, together with his shovel hat, gives him the appearance of an enormous, blunt-headed insect. The scalloped tails, folded like wings around his narrow hips, seem ready at any moment to open out and carry him buzzing over the rooftops.

The coat is at least eighteen inches too long for him and cut in a style which has not been fashionable in the English-speaking world for half a century. Perhaps he inherited it from a tall uncle, or bought it from a gentleman who had no further use for it. Perhaps he borrowed it or picked it up by accident at a coach house and was a hundred miles away before realising his mistake.

It's obvious from the neatness of the stitching and the stiffness of the collar that the garment was made for a man of expensive (if sombre) tastes, who would not have worn it with patched green stockings, as Mr Sculley is in the habit of doing.

There is something indefinably creepy about it, a dim but palpable air of impropriety that may owe something to the whiff of preserving alcohol that accompanies Mr Sculley on his travels and is partly to blame for the gloomy pallor of his skin.

The sight of the frockcoat flapping around his tapered calves reminds Mrs Thrupp of the Wesleyan Women's Temperance League that she once saw a similar coat on the broad shoulders of a ship's surgeon who died of yellow fever in Rio de Janeiro, leaving behind a young wife and two daughters.

It jogs Mrs Sweetwater's memory of a Scottish attorney who was found guilty of embezzlement at Pontefract assizes and transported for seven years to Botany Bay, owing the sickly Mr Sweetwater the sum of sixteen pounds, four shillings and ninepence, which was never paid.

It reminds other people of other things and other places, none of which involves Mr Sculley, but all of which tend to implicate him in some obscurely disreputable business which may or may not involve bodysnatching.

Mr Sculley doffs his hat at the donkey and smiles at the timbercutter, still holding the mouse, and puzzling over their odd behaviour.

~

The admirable Colt with only two Legs was last Week sold to Mr LORD for the Sum of Ten Pounds. Had it not been separated from the Dam, it would doubtless have been preserved a LIVING CURIOSITY; but as it must henceforward be nourished by Cow's Milk, which it receives from a Bottle, its future Prospects must be counted poor.

~

THE INFANT is fast asleep in a cot, its snout protruding from the folds of a coarse blue blanket. According to the battered seaman's clock on the mantle shelf, which was wound in honour of its birth, the creature is a whisker short of two hours old.

Mrs Jakes, having delivered it into the world, and slapped and shaken it, and tipped cod liver oil down its throat, and issued various intructions for its future welfare, is scrubbing her arms in a basin of water. The caul is lying on the floor, folded in a piece of newspaper.

At Mrs Jakes's suggestion, a large square of sailcloth has been hung between two nails, dividing the bed from the rest of the furniture and giving Sarah Dyer and her infant some privacy from prying eyes.

William Dyer is sitting by the fire, gratified by what has taken place under his roof but far from sure what it means. His shoes and socks are steaming by the grate. He stretches out in front of the flames and stares at his feet, as though reconsidering them in the light of recent events and wondering if, from certain angles, they could be said to resemble flippers. Deciding it is impossible to resolve the matter without a bath, he thumbs a plug of tobacco into his pipe and proposes Mrs Jakes join him in a tumbler of rum, which Mrs Jakes declines.

Before he can light his pipe, a dog cart splashes around the corner. It is an old, tatty vehicle, driven by a man whose head has withdrawn completely inside his oilskin. Beside him, sitting bolt upright under a large green umbrella, is Mrs Humphrey, the police magistrate's wife.

The cart slithers to a halt, spraying mud over an oncoming bullock team. The driver's head emerges from his oilskin and he jumps down to assist Mrs Humphrey, who pushes him away with the tip of her umbrella. A short conversation follows, after which Mrs Humphrey walks up the muddy path to the door, watched by Ned and his father. She waits for the door to be opened.

'I am Mrs Humphrey,' she says, nodding civilly to Mrs Jakes but ignoring the others. 'I wish to see the infant.'

'Tis a great honour, ma'am,' cries Sarah Dyer, lifting the pup into bed with her. 'He is only just come out and still a bit shy.'

Mrs Humphrey walks up to the sailcloth and raises the edge with her umbrella before disappearing beneath it, followed by Mrs Jakes. 'Will you allow me to see the child?'

'By all means, ma'am. But you must come closer.' She pulls back the bedsheets far enough for Mrs Humphrey to see the creature's bright eyes and wet snout and quivering whiskers. 'There ma'am. God knows we've done nothing to deserve it.'

Mrs Humphrey gazes at the creature, and then at the mother.

'It's a monster, ma'am, and will suckle me out of my wits. The midwife, Mrs Jakes, God bless her, that pulled it out of me with her bare hands and spanked the life into it, says it must be a miracle, because nature wouldn't allow it otherwise, and I have heard of a Norfolk woman that gave birth to a kitten, only she was drowned for a witch, and the Lord knows I can't swim a stroke and would sooner die in my sleep than give birth to a monster but if God has sent it, ma'am, I cannot turn the mite out.'

Mrs Jakes offers nothing that might confirm or deny her role in the affair.

'Bless us, ma'am, if I didn't almost die of fright at the sight of it, and the poor boy so scared he pissed his breeches,

and all of us save Mrs Jakes praying we wouldn't be struck
down dead for our wickedness.'

'What wickedness is that?' asks Mrs Humphrey, extend-
ing a gloved finger towards the creature's whiskery chin.

'Oh, no wickedness in particular, ma'am, only the
wickedness of the world in general, which is hung
around our necks at birth, such as we must be jeered at
and burnt for saucers, and dug out of our graves by
heathens.'

A gob of milky spittle dribbles into the palm of Mrs
Humphrey's glove.

'Why, ma'am, if you had littluns of your own.'

Mrs Humphrey glances quickly at the boy who has crept
in beside his mother. For a second her face turns crimson.
She draws her hand away. Had the police magistrate,
Adolarius William Horatio Humphrey, been present, he
would have impaled the woman on some Machiavellian
question and denounced her instantly as a fraud. But Mrs
Humphrey is of a different cast of mind from her husband.
She lifts a corner of the blanket and wipes the spittle off
the infant's chops. 'You had no…forewarning?'

'No, ma'am,' cries Sarah Dyer, affronted by the suggestion. She rearranges the blanket so that only the creature's
snout is showing. 'If I'd've known, I'd…lore, ma'am, I
dunno what I'd have done.'

A peremptory grunt announces Mrs Jakes's intention to
leave.

'Wait,' says Mrs Humphrey.

The midwife hesitates. 'I am expected,' she says, without
elaborating. It is not her habit to say more than is necessary, about anything.

'I will not keep you a minute,' says Mrs Humphrey.

Mrs Jakes lifts the sailcloth far enough to see William Dyer tamping his pipe.

'Tell me,' says Mrs Humphrey, choosing her words carefully, 'have you attended other such...deliveries?'

'None of His creatures is alike,' replies Mrs Jakes.

'But this particular infant is...remarkable.'

The midwife signals her guarded agreement with this proposition.

'Indeed, Mrs Jakes, one might go so far as to say it was without precedent.'

'I cannot answer for that.'

'Come now, Mrs Jakes. I dare say there is no such thing recorded in the Bible.'

'You may read as well as I.'

'Better, I think,' snaps Mrs Humphrey.

The midwife glances at William Dyer, who is pretending not to listen, though he is a mere ten feet away. 'If that is all...'

Mrs Humphrey looks past her at the basin of bloody water. She has no doubt that something strange has happened, with or without Mrs Jakes's knowledge. If she has no proof that the laws of Nature have been abused, she has good reason to suspect it. She knows there is nothing made or written that cannot be forged within half a mile of where she is standing. She hears a faint whimper and looks down to see the creature nuzzling for a teat. Sarah Dyer blushes and says, 'Ned will show you out, ma'am, unless you will have some tea.'

Mrs Humphrey smooths the fingers of her gloves and walks briskly to the door.

~

FIRST MEETING of the Van Diemen's Land Scientific Society, held in Mr Sculley's house, Elizabeth Street, on 14th July, 1821, at 7 p.m. Present:

> Major Bell, Acting Engineer and Inspector of Public Works
> Mr Rayner, Inspector of Stock
> Mr Salter, Superintendent of Government Herds
> Mr Hamilton, Assistant Surveyor
> Mr Bent, Publisher of the *Hobart Town Gazette*
> Mr Hacking, Superannuated Pilot
> Mrs Thrupp, Treasurer, Wesleyan Women's Temperance League
> Mrs Sweetwater, Secretary, Van Diemen's Land Horticultural Society
> Mrs Fitzgerald, Schoolmistress

Mr Sculley's parlour is long and narrow, with sooty stains, like bullseyes, on the low ceiling above each sputtering tallow candle. In the middle of the room is a large oak table strewn with instruments that might belong to a watchmaker or surgeon: steel pliers, a hacksaw, a box of lancets, coils of copper wire, some blue and red chalks, the eviscerated organs of a mariner's brass clock. A small black door leads to the study. Next to the door is a tall thin cabinet stacked with jars containing the slack grey bodies of lizards and snakes. The sting of preserving alcohol permeates the room, masking the duller, sweeter odour of putrefaction seeping from the cellar.

There are signs of damage to some of Mr Sculley's

belongings: books torn, jars broken, part of a window boarded up. Recently he returned home from a walk in the woods to find that someone had broken in. A roof panel was caved in, a barrel of biscuits smashed open and the bung knocked out of a cask of vinegar, which spilt its contents all over the stone flags in the cellar. A pair of convict's leather slippers, worn through at the toes, was left behind on a stool, and a pair of Mr Sculley's walking boots stolen. Also missing were two bags of walnuts and half a shoulder of bacon. The thief had opened one of his morocco notebooks and torn out several pages, which Mr Sculley found in his chamber pot, together with an impressive turd.

With the exception of Mr Hacking, the harbour pilot, who lives across the street, none of those attending the meeting has ever set foot in Mr Sculley's house. Some would not have come now but for the presence of Major Bell, whose participation confers a degree of military respectability on the proceedings. Mr Salter, the cantankerous superintendent of herds, arrived under the misapprehension that drink would be provided, and has just discovered his mistake.

Six wooden benches, lent by Mrs Fitzgerald the schoolmistress, are arranged one behind the other along the length of the room, facing a low walnut table draped with a calico sheet. Mr Hacking is seated on the last bench, sucking on his pipe, while the others prowl about, poking their noses into cupboards, opening books and fingering instruments, trying to deduce from the contents of the room what kind of man Mr Sculley is and what he gets up to behind the locked door of his study.

A framed watercolour painting hangs in the sticky halo
of a candle. Mrs Fitzgerald bends forward to look at it.

'The kidney of Major Thomas Bunting,' says Mr Sculley.
He waves his hand bashfully over the sketch. 'A section of
the left organ affected by tuberculosis. Drawn from life.'

'From death, surely,' remarks Mr Hamilton, the assis-
tant surveyor, trying to catch Mrs Sweetwater's eye.

Mr Sculley doesn't hear. He is thinking of his late friend
Major Bunting, of the Royal Marines, who left him the
diseased organ in his will.

'Very pretty,' says Mr Bent.

Mr Sculley smiles modestly. 'I believe,' he says, 'I have
done justice to its owner.'

There are more drawings in a trunk in the corner of the
room: a pig's heart and liver, the pared muscles of an upper
arm and thigh, a human skull and six vertebrae, drawn in
charcoal and red crayon. And the carcass of a dog, turned
inside out like a glove, with each organ carefully numbered.

Mr Sculley's knees will not allow him to stand for long,
so he delivers his lecture—'A Distillation of the Opinions
of Mr Lavater Concerning the New Science of
Physiognomy'—in the musty embrace of a claret armchair.

Mr Salter, sitting by himself, blows his nose loudly and
leans forward on his elbows. 'Who is Lavater?'

'The Reverend Mr Lavater, sir, is a Swiss. He is acknowl-
edged the chief genius among physiognomists. We must
thank that gentleman for elevating this sublime science
above the folly of quacks and fortune-tellers. There are
those who confuse science with superstition, but physiognomy, Mr Salter, is as far from sorcery as philosophy is from
the reading of entrails.'

Several members of the audience glance in the direction of Major Bunting's kidney.

'Do you count yourself a physiognomist?' Mr Rayner inquires gruffly.

'I am a student of that subject. I hold to the principle that a man's moral powers, his passions and sympathies, his affections and repulsions, are depicted on his countenance, and that contemplation of that exterior organ will reveal the life and, as it were, the contractions of the spirit within.'

Mrs Thrupp raises her hand. 'May we assume, sir, that the theory applies equally to the finer sensibilities of the female spirit?'

'Indeed, ma'am, the application of the physiognomical principle is universal. Is it not our inclination to appraise all things by their exterior manifestation, that is, by their physiognomy? Does the sailor, before leaving port, not judge the mood of the sea by its countenance? Does the butcher not reckon the quality of his meat by its physiognomy, its exterior? And the sculptor his stone? Do we not pronounce upon a mug of ale by its appearance? Are we not accustomed, by habit and education, to use our eyes to deduce those inner properties which would otherwise be concealed from us?'

An interjection from Mr Salter. 'Do you propose, sir, that we inspect the conscience of a hog before eating it?'

'Must I vouch for the honesty of my barley?' demands Mr Rayner.

'You misunderstand my analogy, gentlemen,' replies Mr Sculley. 'My point is this: what knowledge is there, of which mankind is capable, that is not in some degree modified by the evidence of our eyes? The physical properties of a sphere can be defined by mathematics, but can we apprehend its inner perfection without seeing it? How then can we exclude the character and soul of mankind from such scrutiny?'

The door opens and in walks Colonel Davey, his boots caked in cow muck. It is clear to all that he has been drinking. Mrs Thrupp frowns. Davey looks around, staggers and sits down heavily beside Major Bell.

Mr Sculley regards the bloated, bloodshot face as though it constituted some particularly artless betrayal of what lay behind it. 'There never existed a profound thinker, or a man of fortitude and prudence, with weak, high eyebrows. Very fleshy lips are the infallible sign of sensuality and indolence; the cut-through, sharp-drawn lip denotes anxiety and avarice. Blue eyes are, invariably, more significant of weakness and effeminacy than brown. Long teeth are proof of weakness and pusillanimity.'

'What of nostrils?' Mr Bent, the printer, inquires mischievously. 'What can you deduce from them?'

A pause, as Mr Sculley sifts through his notes. 'Small nostrils are an indubitable sign…if you'll pardon me…an indubitable sign of…yes, sir, of timidity. The open, breathing nostril, by contrast, is a certain sign of sensibility.'

Mrs Fitzgerald, the pedagogue, raises her arm and says, 'These are assertions, Mr Sculley. You must demonstrate the truth of them. You must persuade us with evidence, not enthusiasm.'

'I intend to, madam,' the old man replies warmly. He turns to Hacking, the pilot, and invites him to remove the calico sheet from the table.

Underneath are two plaster heads. The face of one is grotesquely swollen, with pendulous ear lobes and bulging eyes. A posthumous growth of stubble has sprouted on the chin and half a dozen black eyelashes are embedded in the white plaster. A tuberous nose hangs from the brow like the snout of a sea elephant.

The other face is thin and drawn, with sharp cheek-bones and a high forehead, a beaked nose and square smooth chin. The lips don't quite meet over the jutting teeth. There is something effeminate about the ears.

The audience begins to fidget. Mrs Thrupp and Mrs Sweetwater consider the propriety of leaving, and the propriety of staying, and decide they owe it to Mrs Fitzgerald (who shows no sign of leaving, and is deep in conference with Mr Rayner) to stay.

Mr Sculley allows the murmuring to die down. 'Forgive me for startling you,' he says, 'but could there be any clearer evidence of the qualities that distinguish the man of honour from the common felon?' He reaches for the larger cast and holds it up like a prize cabbage. 'See here, madam, the capacity for cruelty in the forehead, the predisposition to violence in the eyebrows.' He catches Mr Rayner's eye. 'Regard, sir, the lack of compassion in the jaw, the tendency to cowardice in the lips.'

'And who are these unfortunate subjects?' asks Mrs Thrupp.

'The creature in my grasp, madam, is William McGuire, who was hanged a fortnight ago for the murder of his wife. The other is my dear friend, Major Thomas Bunting of the Royal Marines, whose kidney you may observe on the wall.'

'I know Bunting,' mumbles Colonel Davey. 'He owes me a guinea.'

Mr Sculley blinks and removes his spectacles, but before he can speak Mr Salter stands up and approaches the table. 'How fortunate that their characters are known to you,' he says waspishly.

'I beg your pardon?'

The herdsman picks up Major Bunting's head with something less than the reverence it deserves. 'I mean, is the good major's forehead graciously formed because he is a gentleman, or is he a gentleman because his forehead is graciously formed? Is it his countenance that marks him for an officer, or his uniform?' He puts down the major's head. 'To be blunt, sir, has your physiognomy ever sniffed out a homicide that was not already hanged for murder?'

Mr Sculley scrambles out of his armchair to save his late friend from further indignity. 'You are a mocker, Mr Salter. Mockery is the enemy of true science.'

'And what of false science?' inquires Salter.

'You assume truth is absolute, Mr Salter. It is not. What was true to Aristotle is not true to us. The truth in Amsterdam is not inexorably the truth in this room. Could you undertake to explain a kangaroo to a man who had never set foot outside Oxford? Will you believe me if I assure you there exists in New South Wales a bird that laughs like a jackass? Science, sir, is unravelling a world that we have twisted into knots by our own superstition. I believe there is nowhere more conducive to its study than this island, where we may discover nature's strangeness at its source.'

He stops, suddenly conscious that his audience has fallen silent. Mr Salter has a chastened look on his face which passes, by osmosis, to his fellow hecklers, Mr Bent and Mr Rayner. For a moment it seems as though Mrs Fitzgerald will rise from her seat and applaud. Colonel Davey prods Major Bell with his riding crop and grunts, 'Where is Bunting?'

'I wonder...' says Mr Sculley, feeling the blood rush to his cheeks, 'I wonder...'

He is rescued by a knock at the door. All heads turn around as Mr Hacking accepts the invitation to answer it. The door opens and the police magistrate's wife, a woman not known for her devotion to science, enters the room. She acknowledges the respectful smiles of the gentlemen, several of whom appear excessively eager to have her seated beside them.

Mrs Humphrey resists these invitations and walks to the front, where Mr Sculley is mopping his brow with a handkerchief, too flustered to manage a formal introduction. She recognises at once the bulbous head of William McGuire, whose clumsy hanging her husband insisted on recounting over dinner. She is surprised to see beside it the head of Major Bunting, a man she once thought beguiling. Turning away from these macabre exhibits, she waits for the audience to fall silent. 'Are you aware,' she asks, 'that something monstrous has been conceived in our midst?'

Mrs Thrupp and Mrs Sweetwater blush so intensely that Mr Sculley's speckled dome burns in sympathy, while the others assume shades variously suggestive of insouciance, agitation and merriment.

'What, er, manner of monster?' asks Mr Sculley, afraid the meeting is about to be overwhelmed by scandal.

Mrs Humphrey pauses before answering. 'A runt of a seal, delivered to a convict woman this afternoon.'

The audience starts. There are looks of shock on the ladies' faces and ribald disbelief on the gentlemen's. The plaster head of William McGuire appears to smirk. Mrs Sweetwater, being marginally younger than the other ladies and not beyond hopes of child-bearing, utters a little whimper that seems certain to herald a fainting fit, but is pulled back from the brink by the powerful right arm of Mrs Thrupp. Mrs Fitzgerald climbs to her feet but, finding it impossible to articulate the turbid current of her thoughts, sits down again.

Colonel Davey is the first to speak, barking a ferocious 'HA!' and slapping his thigh so forcefully that Mr Sculley topples backwards as if shot.

Emboldened by this display of military scorn, and not averse to an alliance with the disgraced lieutenant-governor, Mr Salter stands up and inquires if the father was also a seal.

Mrs Humphrey fixes him with a stare that would shrivel a more susceptible mind. 'If he was, Mr Salter, he has not seen fit to claim his offspring.'

It is left to Mr Sculley to bring some rigour to the interrogation. 'And you witnessed the event, madam?'

'No, Mr Sculley, I regret to say I did not. But I have seen the infant and interviewed the mother.'

'And you, er, believe…that is to say, you consider it to be…genuine?'

Mrs Humphrey has no intention of pronouncing one way or the other on its genuineness. She has seen things that were genuine and didn't look it, and things that were not genuine and did. She has no great faith in science to sort out the real from the fake, but would rather put Mr Sculley on the scent than her husband, who would go after it with irons and a stockwhip, as he went after William McGuire. 'I had thought you gentlemen would be able to tell me that,' she says.

~

From the best Conjectures that can be formed upon the present Appearance of the Two-Legged Colt, there is much Reason to hope this coura-geous Biped will surmount its irregular Mode of Rearing, and attain its natural Size, which must doubtless be much stunted by the Want of Exercise. Until Monday last, Milk was its only Nutriment, but since then it receives Biscuits and other Food, and may be expected to enlarge its Diet daily.

~

A PERSONAL invitation to observe the inaugural meeting of the scientific society sits for a week on the Reverend Mr Kidney's desk, together with a handwritten note from Mrs Sweetwater signalling her own likely attendance. He would now find it hard to look at her without thinking of bricks. The almost imperceptible swelling of his glands has convinced him that the short uphill walk from his own cottage to Mr Sculley's would set back his fragile conva-lescence.

He is sitting at his desk gazing into the columns of his ledger, as if by staring at the numbers he can cause them

to reveal a surplus where he can only see deficits. A sullen
fire is crackling and spitting in the grate. He leans back in
his chair and pours himself a large brandy, then another,
until his eyes grow heavy and his cheeks blaze and he feels
obliged to close the book.

Mr Kidney's debts have an elemental rhythm, like the
tides. They rise to a certain level, driven by improvident
spending and feckless judgment, and then—just as they're
about to overwhelm him—they subside. He is aware of the
charity that keeps him solvent, and the cost of accepting
it. He resents the calculating benevolence of his financiers:
the loans ostentatiously forgiven, the money orders pressed
into his hand by unscrupulous merchants and boorish farmers who believe that the road to heaven is a tollpath.

His own cottage is secretly mortgaged to Mr Edward
Lord by the terms of an unwitnessed agreement kept in a
padlocked chest in Mr Lord's house near Norfolk Plains.
Mr Kidney looks forward grimly to the day when one
of Lord's servants arrives with a letter informing him
that, due to circumstances beyond his control, Mr Edward
Lord is obliged to request prompt repayment of the loan.
(Thus, he muses, does a servant of the Lord find himself
mortified by a servant of Mr Lord.) When that happens he
will have no choice but to throw himself on the charity of
some other patron, under still more galling terms, and so
on until God chooses to release him from his earthly debts.

In the meantime the chaplain endeavours to be courte-
ous to Mr Lord, who wears black boots up to his knees and
carries a pistol and cane, has a boil the size of a pigeon's
egg under his left ear, and is good for eight thousand pounds
of fresh meat every quarter for the commissariat meat store.

Mr Lord, for his part, never fails to convey his satisfaction at the knowledge that he could at any time, and at the slightest provocation, make the terms of the mortgage public, or introduce some facetious variation, merely for his own amusement.

The chaplain endures these humiliations as the onerous price of bringing the Bible to those who are interested only in profit. He forgets that his motives in coming to Van Diemen's Land were essentially speculative, that his disappointment now is in direct proportion to the ambitions he had when setting out. He never expected to become rich, but he hoped God would allow him to be prosperous. Reputation, he felt certain, could not exist in such a place without money. God, however, was content to see him a beggar and Mr Kidney, since he could do nothing to improve the situation, was forced to make the most of it.

A puckish flame spurts from the coals, illuminating the contents of his crystal decanter and reminding the chaplain that the cask from which it came is almost empty. He draws the marbled ledger towards him and fastens the brass clasp (an unnecessary precaution, since Mrs Jakes is well aware of where his money goes). He shakes a white cotton handkerchief from his pocket and lays it flat on his head. It feels like an angelic hand resting on his scalp. In this beatific state he sits with his hands clasped over his belly, watching the moon climb through the clouds.

The chaplain's study is a misshapen rectangle with a single window set crookedly into the wall, giving an odd slant to the world outside, as if the island were sinking under the weight of convicts being dumped there. The window is kept shut to prevent thieves climbing in or out, so the

room is permanently musty, with dark streaks on the wallpaper and clumps of mould growing in the plaster cornices.

The wallpaper was a gift from the Bishop of Calcutta,
dispatched in a cargo of Bengal rum and sandalwood—a
graceful design of twisted vines of ivy, adorned with red
roses and violets, but only enough for two walls. Did the
bishop imagine that he lived in a cell? 'Your kindness and
concern,' Mr Kidney wrote back, 'are a constant blessing.
Without them, I should consider myself isolated indeed.'
He signed the letter and added a postscript. 'Were it possible to obtain, without inconvenience, a further two rolls of
the same design, I should be infinitely obliged.'

Three months later a stern rebuke arrived from the
bishop. 'I was not aware that your private residence was so
commodious. The impression of indulgence in a minister
of the church is to be avoided at all costs.'

The chaplain concluded from this prickly correspon-
dence that several rolls had in fact been pilfered—a
common enough occurrence—and spent several weeks
sniffing around the dingy shops and warehouses along
Argyle Street, without success.

The bare walls at either end of his study emphasise the
profusion of furniture, mostly of poor quality and nearly
all of it in an advanced state of decay due to the damp.

Along one wall is a tall mahogany bookcase packed with
mildewed volumes by Fielding and an assortment of Bibles:
Brown's family Bible, folio bound; the Catholic Bible, ditto
bound; the quarto Bible bound; Henry's Bible, quarto
bound; Cooke's, Clark's and Wesley's Bibles; as well as three
volumes of Gibbon's *Decline and Fall of the Roman Empire* (the
rest having been eaten by worms on the voyage).

On one side of the bookcase is a threadbare velvet sofa; on the other a high-backed armchair sprouting tufts of horsehair. Squeezed into the remaining corners are an Indian teak sideboard missing one of its door panels (a gift from Mr Birch, the whale baron, who couldn't find a use for it) and a glass-fronted display cabinet containing various pieces of china, several chipped vases, a small blue-glass perfume bottle, a brass Buddha with a startling likeness to Mrs Jakes and three porcelain figurines representing thin, well-dressed English gentlemen. One is reading a newspaper, another is clutching a riding whip and the third is smoking a long-stemmed clay pipe which has lost its bowl.

A floorboard creaks in the hall. The chaplain hears heavy footsteps. The squeak of a hinge that needs oiling. He plucks the angelic handkerchief from his scalp. The door to his study opens and Mrs Jakes floats into the glare of his candle. She is startlingly bare-headed. Her frizz of grey hair is pulled back in a bun so tight that it appears cast in lead.

She looks around his study, as if to confirm that the room is as she left it—furniture unmoved, pockets of dust undisturbed—and remarks, 'I was not expecting you back so soon.' She smells brandy and sees the empty glass on his desk. 'Are you indisposed?'

He glances at the clock on the sideboard. It is a few minutes before eight o'clock. The scientific meeting, if he were to change his mind, is barely under way. He stifles a yawn. 'No more than I deserve after my exertions.'

'Then you'll be wanting dinner?'

'If there is dinner prepared, I will have it.'

'There is not.'

'In that case I shall have a cold supper.' He scrapes the oily strands of his hair until they form crisp black quotation marks behind his ears.

'There is only cold mutton,' says Mrs Jakes.

'Cold mutton will do.'

'It is mostly bones.'

'Even so, I am sure it will serve its purpose. I have not much appetite this evening.'

Mrs Jakes nods. She wonders how long he has been sitting there. 'There is no sauce,' she says.

'Never mind sauce. The mutton will be sufficient on its own.' The chaplain unfastens the brass clasp, as if to resume his work. 'I suppose we have bread?'

Mrs Jakes is not sure if there is bread in the house or how much of it there is or what state it's in. 'I dare say there is something.'

'Then something will have to do.' His nose twitches at the strange smell in the room, a pungent blubbery smell not unlike the kind that hangs around sealers' pubs, mixed with beer and shag tobacco. He is tempted to ask Mrs Jakes where she has been but knows he would not get a straight answer.

Mrs Jakes has made it plain over the years that she is answerable to him only in her capacity as housekeeper. She will discuss household matters—the price of mutton, the availability of soap, the recalcitrance of tradesmen—but keeps her private affairs to herself.

An equanimity exists between them, rooted in long familiarity and mutual suspicion. If a suggestion of affection, and even dependence, has been kindled out of this sceptical intimacy, neither the chaplain nor his housekeeper will acknowledge it.

The Reverend Mr Kidney knows about and has given tacit consent to her work as a midwife. Mrs Jakes, having once gained this consent, has never given him the opportunity to qualify it. She leaves the cottage without asking and returns when it suits her. She receives anxious visitors at the kitchen door, usually after dark, and often departs with them, carrying her canvas sack over her shoulder.

On such nights, when there is no moon, he leaves a candle burning at a parlour window. It serves no useful purpose and has often burnt itself out by the time Mrs Jakes returns. The candle is never mentioned between them. Both would find it awkward to explain the greasy smudge on the sill.

Mr Kidney abandons the pretence of consulting his ledger and says, 'I did not go to the scientific meeting.'

'I guessed as much.'

'Matters here required my attention.'

She glances at the mess of papers on his desk. 'No doubt.'

'I visited the bridge this afternoon,' continues the chaplain. 'I fear I may have caught another chill.'

Mrs Jakes offers no comment but raises her eyebrows by the amount needed to remind him that she has in her trunk various foul-tasting potions and noxious ointments guaranteed to bring relief from any ailment.

He stands to draw the curtains. 'I trust your own afternoon was satisfactory.'

It crosses Mrs Jakes's mind to mention the birth of the seal pup, but as this would set an undesirable precedent in their domestic intercourse she decides against it.

The chaplain knows better than to inquire further. He opens the top drawer of his desk and slides the marbled ledger under a pile of documents. 'I intend to retire straight after supper. My circulation is not yet recovered.'

Mrs Jakes nods. 'Is that all?' she asks.

~

IF THE rumour could be tagged and followed, like a cow with a bell around its neck, it would go like this:

Mary Blunden, assigned servant to Mrs Humphrey, the police magistrate's wife, overhears a ticket-of-leave man swear to having witnessed a monstrous birth. Mary Blunden is too frightened to want to see the creature for herself, but is told by John Triggs, who shod the horses for Mr Trelawny's barouche, that the surgeon has been summoned to discover the nature of a horrid thing born to a convict woman in a hovel in Argyle Street.

John Triggs can't say for certain what the surgeon saw, or if he came at all, but he knows for sure that the creature was inhuman and deformed and is a punishment for some wicked perversion, the mother being a gypsy woman, according to Ann Hammond, wife of the magistrate's clerk, and gypsies known for their depravity. Mary Blunden recounts the story word for word, with some fancy embellishments of her own, to her friend Amy Dodden, wife of James Dodden the wharfinger.

Amy Dodden repeats the story to her husband, at least what she can remember of it, with some details that were missing from the original, such as how the creature was born without eyes and had a black spot on its rump and webbed hands.

James Dodden eats his boiled bacon and potatoes in

silence, then wanders off for an hour with his pipe, which carries him by habit past the door of James Ellis, ship's chandler and dealer in stolen goods. The door is ajar and the wharfinger's nostrils catch at the smell of mulled ale simmering on the stove.

Dodden invites himself in with the excuse of informing the chandler about a consignment of duck frocks and linen shirts just arrived on a sloop from Sydney. But the ale goes to his head and he starts telling Ellis about the monster that sprang from an Egyptian's loins in Argyle Street and wasn't one sex or the other but both at once.

Ellis doesn't believe a word of it, but relates it an hour later to a shovel-bearded, mud-spattered, yellow-skinned figure bearing some faint resemblance to a description of Daniel Septon, who absconded from Hobart gaol two months ago and was last sighted by a constable in the scrub near New Norfolk, and has five pounds on his head that nobody is anxious to claim.

The shovel-bearded figure listens while he warms his bones in front of the fire. Then he slips away into the darkness, stuffing his knapsack with tobacco and sugar and flour and dry gunpowder, which he pays for with a silver watch stolen from Mr Mossop, the harbourmaster.

So the rumour splits in two. Half rides away, on a stolen black mare, to the Barley Mow Inn at Black Snake, ten miles away. It's retold, at the end of a loaded pistol, to a drunken constable, who is forced to hand over his boots and is left tied by the wrists and ankles to a sassafras tree.

The other half wanders home with James Dodden, pausing to ingratiate itself with the drunken soldiers in the Bird-in-Hand, who share it with their mates in the guardhouse, who use it to frighten the whores loitering by the harbour, who whisper it to the sailors and the sealers and the husky hollow-eyed ticket-of-leave men for three-pence a time, in the rain, up against a wall.

The morning after, it finds its way into the flapping ears of shopkeepers and settlers' wives on their way to church, and is picked up by whalers in the harbour and widows shuf-fling around the cemetery, who declare that they are not surprised, as gypsy women are notorious for their filthy habits and would steal an honest woman's husband the minute her back was turned, and her children into the bargain.

While the rumour is doing its rounds, Mrs Fitzgerald is administering the final improvements to her face before setting out in search of Mr Sculley, whom she finds fossick-ing under the leaves of his rhubarb plants. 'Good morning,' she says. 'I am surprised to see you here.'

'Indeed,' replies Mr Sculley. 'Did you expect me to be breakfasting with the seal pup?'

The schoolmistress eyes him coolly under the rim of her black bonnet. 'I supposed that you might be on your way to church.'

'Forgive me. I did not mean to sound impertinent, but Mr Kidney will have to do without my attendance this morning. I intend to call on the parents of the creature and am hopeful of securing an interview.'

'Then you believe Mrs Humphrey to be correct in her assertions?'

The old gentleman emerges from the rhubarb holding a lizard by the tail. 'I believe she saw what she says she saw. I cannot speculate on whether the phenomenon occurred as it was reported to her.'

Mrs Fitzgerald's own instincts incline her to suspect fraud. She emerges warily from under her umbrella. 'You appear sceptical, Mr Sculley.'

'Not sceptical, madam. Cautious.' He subjects the lizard to a cursory examination before letting it go. 'Science is an empirical study and must not be confused with credulity.'

'I hope I am not credulous.'

'On the contrary, I consider you to be the most incredulous of women. But we must not jump to conclusions. Science has given us sound reasons for postponing judgment on matters beyond our experience.'

Mrs Fitzgerald, who had hoped to be solicited for an opinion, now feels relieved not to have given it. 'Then you do not deny the possibility?'

'Certainly not. If science teaches us anything, it teaches us to contemplate the possibility of everything, and the certainty of nothing. Are we not standing upright at the bottom of the world, when our forebears would have had us falling off?'

The schoolmistress, glancing down at her feet, concedes that this is so.

'If it is fraud,' continues Mr Sculley, 'we must endeavour to expose it. We cannot do that until we have properly inspected the evidence.' He looks intently at Mrs Fitzgerald, as if deciding whether to reveal a confidence, then lowers his voice. 'Of course, madam, from a scientific point of view, such aberrations are only to be expected.' The slightest hint of a gasp encourages him to go on. 'The study of physiognomy must dispose us to apply its principles to the world of nature. The creature, if its authenticity can be proven, is no less indicative of the character of this place than a homicide's brow is proof of his tendencies. They are both signs and we need but the ability to read them.'

'Why, sir, you appear almost delighted by the event.'

'Not delighted, madam, but not dismayed.'

The schoolmistress glances at the lizard, which has not moved since its release and now gives every appearance of being dead. 'And the Almighty. What are we to make of His part in it?'

'That,' says Mr Sculley, looking down the hill towards the chaplain's cottage, 'is for Mr Kidney to fathom.'

~

We have this Afternoon received Information that the Banditti, which have been for so long in the Woods of this Island committing Murders and Robberies, have had their Number augmented by Absconders from the Settlement in Port Dalrymple, whose Determination to emulate the Outrages of their Companions has occasioned much Grief for the honest Inhabitants of Jericho and Tea-Tree Brush.

~

AT A quarter past six, Mrs Jakes opens her eyes. It is still dark outside and silent except for the distant cry of a deranged rooster that has been crowing throughout the night. Mrs Jakes sits up and rubs her eyeballs, folds back the woollen blankets, yawns and swings her legs over the side of the bed.

There is frost on the windows, growing out from the corners in sharp white triangles. The Reverend Mr Kidney is snoring loudly in the next room. Mrs Jakes shuffles to the kitchen in her nightshirt and slippers and rustles the still-warm embers of the fire with a poker.

The logs flare up, casting lurid shadows on the walls. Mrs Jakes makes herself a pot of tea, cuts the bruises out of a worm-eaten apple, picks at the knuckle of a bacon bone, then pads back to her bedroom to get dressed.

There are cobwebs hanging from the beams which Mrs Jakes has never seen fit to brush away. The spiders go about their business without fear of being disturbed, littering her floor with the hollow, desiccated corpses of moths and blowflies.

The rough plaster walls are bare and whitewashed. A padlocked wooden trunk sits at the bottom of her bed, next to a dressing-table with a tarnished oval mirror that contains everything Mrs Jakes can remember of her life.

Trapped in its dusty glass is the image of a plainly dressed woman, perhaps twenty years old, bending over the naked body of a man much older than herself, bare feet splayed on the end of a carpenter's bench. The man's skin is grey and his neck long and scrawny like a chicken's. His right hand is ringed with calluses. The left thumb is hammered almost flat. A red diagonal scar runs across the bridge of his nose.

The woman shaves his beard and scrubs his fingernails and snips the hairs in his ears. She wraps his throat in a brown woollen scarf to cover the bruise and pulls a pair of ragged trousers along his skinny legs. Then she puts a jacket on him and combs the sawdust out of his hair and pushes a daisy into his buttonhole. The dead man is her husband, John Jakes, who was hanged for stealing a ram.

It is a quirk of memory that John Jakes hardly ever comes to her alive, but dead he cannot keep away, lying there with his rueful half-smile, and a lump in his broken neck, as if to remind her that stealing the ram was her idea.

Beyond this image is another one, of a stouter, middle-aged woman with a mob-cap pulled over her grey hair, in a sparsely furnished room at the top of a narrow stair-case, with an iron bed and wooden table and two plain chairs, and a basin of bloody water on the floor. A young woman is sobbing on the bed. The door opens and a burly constable, flanked by two medical gentlemen, announces the arrest of Mrs Jakes, the abortionist.

～

BLOOD. GALLONS of it. Enough to stain the harbour red. Crowds of men on the beach with flecks of scarlet spume shivering in their whiskers. The sand streaked like a butcher's apron. Two whales dragged out and cut open on the deck of the *Jupiter* and another one lashed to the side with ropes. The *Martha* leaking blood from every sump and sinkhole. Men and boats tangled up in streaky red ribbons. The stink of boiling blubber blowing across from the try-pots. And the richest man in Van Diemen's Land, Mr Birch, standing on the shingle in his shiny black shoes, clutching his stovepipe hat with one hand while he holds out the other one for shaking. Wiping the froth off his moustache while he reckons the weight of blubber on board.

The Reverend Mr Kidney surveys the rows of empty

pews in his ramshackle wooden church. A dozen worshippers are huddled together, sullen faces buried in their mildewed hymn books. As the chaplain attempts to squeeze out another hymn, the south door opens. A man dressed in moleskins and calico smock enters, bends down, and whispers to the man nearest him about the queer thing born the night before. The second man gathers up his felt hat and canvas bag and they slip away.

The singing fades and the chaplain inspects what remains of his congregation: six men, five women and an invalid child wrapped in a rug. The rest are standing on the beach, watching the whalers at work. The boats have been out since dawn, flouting the Sabbath as they do every year, if the bonus is big enough. Smoke from the try-pots wafts through the half-open door and hangs like mist around the high windows. From time to time the crack of a musket dawdles around the bays.

The chaplain leans forward, his round red face jutting out of the pulpit. He has no intention of wasting a new sermon on such a meagre congregation, but slips his notes under the Bible lying open on the lectern and begins instead to extemporise on the subject of duty, and especially the grave necessity of observing the Sabbath, which is the gift of the Almighty and not something to be bought off for a shilling. He is barely into his stride when the invalid child throws off her rug and starts limping away. As the child's mother hurries after her, the door creaks. An ancient woman in a black shawl advances a couple of steps into the church, then stops. The chaplain directs her to sit down, but the woman stands her ground.

'Ain't you heard, sir?'

Those worshippers not dulled into sleep by the sermon look at her expectantly.

The old crone hitches the shawl over her shoulders. 'A poor hussy's give birth to a MONSTER!'

~

A curious Report has reached us concerning the Two-Legged Pony. In this eccentric Creature a new Phenomenon begins to make its Appearance in a SPIRAL TUMOUR shooting out between the Ears, and which, should it arrive to any Length, will give a lively Representation of the UNICORN; but it is more probable this may proceed from a Bruise on the Forehead than from any further Design of Nature to astonish her Admirers.

~

IT DOESN'T take long for a crowd to gather, buttoned up in their sharp collars and Sunday suits, babbling and jostling for the best view. Men with cinders in their beards and blood-spattered collars. Women murmuring under leaky umbrellas. Dogs scratching fleas out of their ribs.

'How many now?' asks Sarah Dyer, brushing her hair behind the sailcloth. 'Is there any gentry among 'em?'

'Only Mr Trelawny,' says Ned, keeping watch at the window.

'Pish,' she says. 'Trelawny ain't gentry.'

Forty-four citizens have come to pay their respects: sixteen wives and widows, five maidservants, eleven ticket-of-leave convicts, a red-haired corporal and three privates, seven children, two horses, three dogs and Trelawny the surgeon, perched on the double-sprung green leather seats of his barouche, ordering the crowd to part, like Moses commanding the Red Sea. And William Dyer standing there in his patched Sunday coat, arms folded, smoke dribbling out of him, blocking the door.

'I am a physician,' shouts Trelawny. 'I must be allowed to see the patient.'

The black cylinder of his stovepipe hat bobs through the crowd while the corporal barks orders: 'Move yerselves, gents—step aside, missus—mind yer elbows.' Finally Trelawny emerges from the fray, swinging his stick like a man beating a dog from his ankles. 'If you are the master of this dwelling,' he tells Dyer, 'I demand to be admitted.'

'What's your father doing now?' hisses Sarah Dyer.

'He's talking to Trelawny,' says Ned.

The surgeon, realising that money will have to change hands if he is to gain entry, wrestles with his purse. He presses a coin into Dyer's palm. Then another. Dyer waits for a third, but the purse vanishes as quickly as it was produced. 'Much obliged, sir,' he mumbles. 'The missus'll be grateful.'

The door opens. Trelawny walks in, looks about the room and clamps his handkerchief to his nose. He scowls at the boy, as if some monstrous family tendency were equally visible in him, and says, 'Where's the patient?'

'There ain't one,' Sarah Dyer calls from behind the sail-cloth.

There are leech scabs on the doctor's ears and on the backs of his hands, and a fresh sore on his neck which he keeps dabbing with his handkerchief. His wet lips twitch like suckers.

'Mam's in bed,' says Ned.

Trelawny stuffs the hanky back in his pocket and follows his hat under the sailcloth. 'Is that the infant?' he asks, pointing with his stick at the wheezing bundle in the cot.

'Indeed, sir,' says Sarah, peeling back a corner of the blanket to reveal the creature's glossy head and whiskers.

Trelawny snatches the infant out of the cot and satisfies himself that it conforms to the external description of a seal pup. 'And you claim to have given birth to this…thing?'

'I never claimed nothing, sir. I know it.'

'Sit up, woman.'

'Bless me, sir,' says Sarah, hoisting herself upright. 'I am hardly fit to be inspected by a gentleman.'

Trelawny snorts and tells her to pull up her smock as he has paid two shillings for the privilege of looking at her.

'You will be gentle, sir?'

'I will be more gentle than the magistrate.'

Before long Sarah Dyer is whimpering and Trelawny is telling her to stop squirming and put her foot on his shoulder and she cries out, 'Don't hurt me, doctor, I won't have no forceps,' and Trelawny snaps at her to hold her tongue dammit and keep still.

Finally Trelawny withdraws from her smock. 'Has the midwife attended you since the birth?'

'No, sir.'

'And no-one else has come near you?'

'Not a soul, sir, not even me 'usband.'

'Then you have not been…interfered with?'

'Interfered with?'

'Never mind.'

The crowd outside is getting fidgety. William Dyer is obliged to sacrifice thruppence to the constable to keep the peace. Mrs Dyer hastily rearranges her garments and shakes a rug over her lap.

'If there is fraud in this, madam,' says Trelawny, 'I shall find it out. I shall find it out and turn you over to the magistrate.' He dabs his mouth on his sleeve. 'If there is fraud you will pay for it.'

'Fraud, sir? There is no fraud in it. You may ask Mrs Jakes. If there was any fraud Mrs Jakes would have found it out.'

His lips ripple like the skirt of a snail prised from a rock. 'I cannot tell the truth of the matter,' he says, 'without an examination of the fallopian tubes.'

'Heaven knows, sir, you may send a chimneysweep's boy up there if you desire but I doubt what good it'll do now the thing is born.' She cups an ear to the crowd outside. 'Praise God, sir, a woman's womb is a blessed thing and only He knows what'll come out of it and how many heads it'll have and who's to say what's normal, sir, when we're banished here with naked savages and will never see London again and there's unicorns growing in the woods with half their legs missing and what'll He send us next?'

'Enough,' shouts Trelawny. 'Do not imagine, madam, that you have heard the last of this.'

'Indeed, sir, I should be sorry to think so as I hope the child will have a long life.'

He packs away his instruments, re-attaches his hat and departs without another word.

'There now, boy,' says Mrs Dyer, brushing her hair

around her ears. 'The doctor has done his business. You may tell your father to let the others in.'

~

THE REVEREND Mr Kidney shuts the church door behind him and squints against the sunshine. He has seen miscreations before—infants without limbs, without eyes, with cleft palates or ears like mushrooms—presented to him matter-of-factly for burial. If some unfortunate convict woman has now given birth to a monstrosity, he has no wish to see it until he's sent for, which he undoubtedly will be tomorrow or the next day, when its life is extinguished.

He locks the door with a heavy iron key. The pre-caution seems superfluous as there is little worth stealing—a bent candlestick and a box of candles, a few pewter goblets and a hundred and seventy-six secondhand hymn books donated by a Methodist congregation in Chesterfield. But even these would vanish if the church was left open.

A crow swoops past and flops onto the ground near his feet. It hops about in the mud and then flaps away into the wrinkled branches of a gum tree, where it sits watching him.

The chaplain's thoughts are on lunch—a leg of lamb basted with lard and sprigs of rosemary, and beans and potatoes from his own garden, with Mrs Jakes's muddy fingerprints baked into their skins.

A little further up the hill he sees Mr Sculley lying in wait for him in the shadow of a small elm, one of dozens grown from seedlings by Mr Hammond, the magistrate's clerk, to remind him of the gardens at Kew.

The chaplain cannot avoid an encounter except by making a detour down Macquarie Street, past the gaol, where he would be obliged to look on the maggoty head of a bushranger ambushed in the woods near Herdsman's Cove. Mr Kidney disapproves of such exhibitions. He considers them barbarous and un-Christian. But his authority, such as it is, does not extend beyond the living, and the most he can do is shut his eyes.

He slackens his pace in the hope that Mr Sculley may get tired of waiting. But the old gentleman is busily inspecting a beetle. The chaplain trudges on until he has no choice but to offer a greeting.

'Mr Kidney,' says Mr Sculley, looking up. 'We missed you at the meeting. Are you ill?'

The chaplain wipes his brow with his handkerchief. 'I am always ill,' he snorts. 'The climate does not agree with me. But thankfully I am less ill than I was.'

Mr Sculley is uncertain whether the chaplain's last assertion calls for sympathy or celebration. He smiles awkwardly. 'My home is not five minutes' walk. Will you allow me to offer you some refreshment?'

'No, thank you,' snaps Mr Kidney, before relenting. 'Perhaps a short visit.'

Mr Sculley wraps the beetle in his handkerchief and slips it in his pocket. He is anxious to hear the chaplain's opinion on the monstrous birth but is unsure how to broach the subject without appearing flippant. 'We had a most stimulating debate last night,' he says. 'The subject was physiognomy.'

'Really,' the chaplain replies without interest. 'I am sorry to have missed it.'

Mr Sculley does not speak again until they are inside the house. 'May I offer you a cup of tea?' he asks. 'Or wine?'

'Perhaps,' says Mr Kidney, affecting great difficulty in choosing between them, 'perhaps a glass of claret.'

The room is dark, despite the sun. A sooty glow illuminates jars filled with brownish liquid, each containing the twisted corpse of an animal. Mr Kidney takes the proffered glass and holds it up to the window, as if to ensure there is nothing floating in it, then sits down beside the bottle.

'Will you allow me to show you some pictures?' asks Mr Sculley, riffling through the pages of Lavater's *Essays on Physiognomy* while the chaplain helps himself to more claret.

At last Mr Sculley finds what he is looking for. He pulls up a chair and holds the book open for Mr Kidney to see. There are six profiles on the page, distinguished by small differences in the shape of the nose and forehead. 'Perhaps you will honour me with your opinion of the first?'

Mr Kidney glances carelessly at the drawing. 'It is a face,' he says. 'I have no opinion as to its merits.'

'But you will acknowledge that the face is a noble one?'

'The owner of it may be noble, or he may be ignoble. I do not see how it is possible to judge.'

'It is a woman's face, but no matter. The principle is the same.'

'The nose is not unattractive,' says the chaplain. 'I don't much care for the chin. But as to the woman's character, I would not be so presumptuous as to form an opinion.'

'But will you not concede the mixture of compassion and courage, of levity and perseverance, of harmony...and nobility of mind, of, er, simplicity and peace? Can you not tell the lack of pretension in the eye, the sincerity of the nose...the powers of memory evident in the forehead...can you not deduce these things simply by observation of the young woman's face?'

'No,' answers Mr Kidney. 'I cannot.'

'But now that I have identified these qualities, you will not dispute them?'

'The woman may be sincere or she may be insincere. I have no grounds for believing that her nose has anything to do with it.'

'That is because you are no physiognomist,' says Mr Sculley. He points to another profile. 'Now, what do you make of the forehead?'

Mr Kidney inspects the portrait for a minute or so. 'It is a round forehead.'

'It is an arched forehead,' Mr Sculley corrects him, 'and it signifies malice. Our gaol is full of arched foreheads. You will not suggest that they are there by accident?'

'Indeed they are not. They are there because the law has put them there. And I believe the law was not pronouncing on the slope of their foreheads.'

'Yet you cannot deny that the slope of their foreheads corresponds precisely with what the law has decreed for them.'

'It may also correspond with the length of their nose, or the colour of their eyes, or the cut of their trousers. But I do not think the magistrate took account of it when passing sentence.'

'But would it not improve matters if he did?'

The chaplain's expression hardens. 'How, sir? Do you expect a person's nose to be taken into evidence? Must a man's jaw be held against him?' He extends a hand towards the claret. 'Science, Mr Sculley, is no way to understand the human soul.'

The old man closes the book. 'Did you know that the blacks on this island have no means of making fire?'

Mr Kidney shrugs to indicate that he was not aware of it, but is not at all surprised.

'And yet, Mr Kidney, they are rarely without fire.'

The chaplain grunts.

'They live in tribes. If the fire of one tribe is extinguished, they must go in search of another tribe to obtain a flame. By law this flame must never be refused, even if the tribes are at war.'

'One mustn't suppose fellow feeling is confined to the European races. I have seen evidence of Christian charity even among savages.'

'Then perhaps, Mr Kidney, you will concede that intelligence and fellow-feeling do not depend upon civilisation, but upon some other facet.'

This is not the first time the chaplain has been subjected to one of Mr Sculley's lectures. The last one was about bees. His gaze drifts back to the bottle. 'Some of the most civilised men of my acquaintance,' he says, 'are the biggest fools.'

'And some of the lowest bred have the most subtle minds?'

Mr Kidney pours more wine into his glass. His face is very red. He leans forward and declares, in a low portentous voice, 'There are riddles, Mr Sculley, that God did not intend us to solve.' He raises the glass to his nose and holds it there as if savouring, for the first time, its singular bouquet of sawdust and sweaty saddles. 'I had thought, sir, that your intention in bringing me here was to discuss the monster in our midst.'

Mr Sculley's eyes open wide. 'No, that is...how?'

'How did I hear of it? Come now, Mr Sculley. A diligent parson must keep his ear to the ground.'

Mr Sculley has never heard the Reverend Mr Kidney referred to as diligent. He offers an unconvincing smile. 'Have you...seen it?'

'Seen it? No, sir. Have you?'

'I have not yet been afforded the privilege.'

'The privilege? Is that what we are to call it?'

'Surely it is always a privilege to observe the wonders of God's creation.'

The chaplain casts his eye over the pale malevolent specimens gaping at him from their glass jars. 'If God is to be credited with its creation.'

'Are we then to presume on His ignorance?'

The Reverend Mr Kidney stands up to leave. 'I am a simple clergyman, Mr Sculley. I leave it to your'—he casts about for a suitably disparaging term—'your physiognomy to discover the truth of the matter.'

~

With Regret we have to mention the Death of the Two-Legged Pony, together with the total Extinction of that prodigious Curiosity, owing to the barbarous Incompetence of the Operator who undertook the Preservation of the Skin by separating it from its perishable Contents. This Performance was taken in Hand by a Journeyman Butcher who, setting to Work in the Proprietor's Absence, and intent upon preserving the Carcass rather than the Hide, dismembered totally the little Animal; cut off the Head, and disfigured it with twenty ghastly Apertures, as a further Testimony of his Skill and Science. The Death of the Creature was attributed to a Change of Diet, a Potation of Barley Meal being substituted in the place of clear Milk, to which it had been accustomed; and the Powers of Digestion, possibly from Want of Exercise, of which it was incapable, being too feeble to admit the Change.

~

NOBODY EXPECTS the thing to live, except its mother. William Dyer keeps peering into the cot to see if it's still breathing. Now and then it makes a strange cry—a kind of yelp, like a beaten dog—but most of the time it just lies there, watching them out of its big round eyes.

Mrs Jakes comes around to see that everything is properly tied off. She bastes the knot with lard to stop it going bad and scrubs the pup's face and smears bacon fat on its flippers. Ned sits by its cot, like a sentry, keeping the blankets tucked in and spooning milk between its lips to prepare it for weaning.

Every morning a crowd gathers outside the door (gap-toothed, runny-nosed, stamping their feet against the cold) to find out if the creature died during the night, and what it's called, and who the father is. They huddle against the chimney, warming themselves against the bricks, and take turns staring through the window.

Mr Trelawny arrives in his barouche with another

gentleman, both reeking of brandy, pecking at the mud with their silver-topped canes. The pair of them disappear behind the sailcloth and spend the afternoon prodding and squeezing, which costs them a sovereign each with nothing to show for it.

The recent and much lamented death of Dr Clooney (crushed by a fallen tree, with hardly a scratch on him) has left the medical profession embarrassed for a second opinion. There's a doctor in Port Dalrymple, on the north coast, but that is a week's ride away and rain has made the road impassable in fifty places. There was a ship's surgeon on the *Hibernia*, which sailed a fortnight ago for Calcutta. Another is expected on the *Prince Leopold*, which has been held up in Port Jackson and will not arrive for three weeks or more. So there is only Trelawny and his friend, Mr Jeremiah Furphy, who was once an apothecary's boy in Chichester and never lost the knack (he says) of mixing up a potion.

The two men spend an hour hunched over the chamber pot, inspecting the creature's evacuations. They peer up one end and down the other. They pluck whiskers from its chin and put callipers around its skull and hold it underwater, and all they can ask is this: was the mother, by any chance, ravaged by a seal while she slept?

'If I was, gentlemen,' cries Sarah, feigning shock, 'I never felt a thing, and never gave my consent to it.'

'Mr Furphy,' says Trelawny, 'I believe it is time you asked the boy some questions.'

'My opinion exactly,' says Furphy, who had not thought of it before now.

'He don't know nothing,' cries Sarah. 'You keep your hands off him.'

But Furphy already has his right hand on the boy's neckerchief. He glances at Trelawny and proceeds to drag Ned outside. 'Well, boy,' says Furphy. 'What do you know?'

'I don't know nothing,' says Ned.

Furphy tightens his grip on the neckerchief.

'Honest, sir, I'd tell you if I knew.'

'Knew what?'

'Anything, sir, only…'

'Only what, boy?'

'Only I saw Mr Armstrong give Mam a plum from the chaplain's tree.'

'Armstrong? The hangman?'

'That's him, sir.'

Furphy lets go of the neckerchief. 'What then?'

'Then Mam asks him in.'

'And?'

'And Mr Armstrong says why don't I fetch some wood for the fire and there's a plum in it for you, boy, only don't hurry back as your mother and me's got business to discuss. I ask him what business and he says grown-ups' business now get along with you. Don't snap at the boy, says Mam, he's only asking. Do you want the plum or don't you, says Mr Armstrong with a lump in his trousers, so I go outside only the latch doesn't fall and the wind blows the door open and I hear the pair of them grunting and Mam hisses the boy'll hear us and Mr Armstrong says let him hear, it won't kill him, and the grunting gets louder and Mam says get on with it, Joshua, for gawdsakes, and suddenly there's a groan like a tree falling and Mr Armstrong is standing in the doorway hitching his pants up.'

Furphy thinks for a while. 'What about the midwife?'
he asks. 'Did she have a hand in it?'

'Yes, sir,' says Ned, 'it was her hand that pulled it out.'

Employing a variation of the skills he learnt in the
apothecary's shop, Mr Jeremiah Furphy attempts to fuse
these snippets of information with others already in his
possession. The resulting amalgam is enough to satisfy him
but not Trelawny, who threatens Ned with a more violent
interrogation before inserting himself summarily into his
stovepipe hat and marching off.

~

Our Readers will doubtless have heard of the
Unusual Delivery that occurred on Saturday last
in Lodgings in Argyle-street. We have now viewed
the Infant and can assert, with little Fear of
Contradiction, that the Creature resembles, in
every Particular save that of Parentage, a healthy
SEAL PUP; which plain Resemblance the Mother
herself will not deny and has been confirmed by
our distinguished Surgeon, Mr TRELAWNY.
Notwithstanding that Gentleman's Opinion, we
must confess that our own Nose strongly inclines
us to smell a RAT.

~

IT IS Mrs Jakes's opinion that all men are fools. She holds
this opinion in the sense that Pythagoras held an opinion
about right-angled triangles and Copernicus about planets.

She would concede (if pressed) that men are fools in different degrees and different guises. But that they are fools Mrs Jakes has no doubt. She sees the proof of it in the police magistrate and Mr Riley the meat inspector and the hare-lipped clerk at the deputy surveyor's office, who claims to have watched the Duke of Wellington smoking a cheroot on Brighton beach; in every wheezing lawyer and bull-necked constable and ham-fisted surgeon. She can't swear that no such thing as a sensible man ever existed or ever would exist; only that she has never met such a man, nor heard of him, except in novels. If sensible men exist, Mrs Jakes thinks they must be found among the Eskimo races, or the Chinese, whose brains have not been scrambled by drink and religion.

She does not believe there is any kind of sense in a savage, or in any race that will not wear trousers. She is kind to blacks all the same, but wary, as she would be with a dog. She gives them food and sometimes a pinch of tobacco from the chaplain's pouch, and one afternoon she cried as she watched a group of them keening over a dead child, refusing to leave until Mr Kidney laid his hand on the tiny corpse. They were more like ghosts than people, dark moaning shapes who cowered at the sight of a horse and did not understand the use of a knife and fork. Mrs Jakes was not entirely sure they were human.

'Ah, Mrs Jakes. I've been trying to find you.'

She looks up from the iron tub in the scullery, where she has spent the past half-hour pounding the chaplain's bed linen. She eyes him coldly before plunging the sheet back in the grey soapy water.

The chaplain is uncertain what to make of her

expression—resentment at his presence in a part of the house which she considers to be her own, or annoyance at the deplorable state of his linen.

The scullery is illuminated by a small square dusty window set low down in the wall. There are numerous pots and jars, whose contents the chaplain can't see, but which he suspects of having some vaguely medicinal purpose. Mrs Jakes is a great one for poultices and the stink in the scullery reminds him of the plasters which she presses on his gouty legs in summer, when they swell up like marrows.

The rain has left puddles of dirty water on the stone floor which he can't avoid standing in. The walls glitter with damp. The chaplain smiles and bends down, as if some interesting sight were suddenly visible through the window, although the dust and cobwebs have made the glass almost opaque.

A dog barks in the distance. The chaplain straightens up. Mrs Jakes hauls the sheet out of the tub and wrings the water out of it.

It is ten days since Sarah Dyer gave birth to her monster. On three occasions Mr Kidney has coaxed himself to within a dozen feet of the crowd gawping from the road, but each time something has held him back, a fear that whatever is inside might be genuine. He is afraid of looking on the creature and feeling not awe at the supreme mystery of God's purpose but dismay at some clever piece of sorcery.

It was his earnest hope that the creature would not live, and that he would not therefore be required to implicate himself in its welfare. Reports, however, have reached his ears that the infant has not merely survived but is thriving.

Mrs Jakes's face, distorted by shadows and framed by

the harsh flaps of her mob-cap, looms over the tub. 'You wish to know about the birth.'

Mr Kidney betrays no surprise at having his thoughts read. He has become accustomed to Mrs Jakes's unusual powers of intuition. 'I understand you had some role in the affair,' he says.

'I delivered the creature.'

'And you attended on the mother before the birth?'

Mrs Jakes nods.

'Then you would have been able to observe any duplicity, any, what shall we say…unnatural preparations?'

She fishes another sheet out of the basket and submerges it beneath the scum. 'Such as?'

The chaplain has only the flimsiest knowledge of female anatomy and is not prepared to subject it to Mrs Jakes's interrogation. He looks over his shoulder and is puzzled to see a seal pelt hanging from a nail behind the door. Seal-skin mittens are a common item in Hobart Town but they are generally bought from shops. He wonders if Mrs Jakes intends to manufacture a pair for herself. 'The process, I dare say, is open to…fraud?'

'Perhaps it is. But a midwife cannot be deceived.'

'You insist that this creature, this offspring, emerged naturally from the woman?'

Mrs Jakes stops rubbing and lets the sheet flop into the water. 'Trelawny saw the caul, didn't he?'

'I have no great faith in Mr Trelawny's perspicacity— nor, I believe, do you.'

The Reverend Mr Kidney does not pretend to know what his housekeeper does on the evenings when she is absent and leaves his supper under a linen teacloth. It has never occurred to him that there might be anything illicit about her business. Nor that the formless infants which are, from time to time, found dead in doorways, or buried under piles of lumber, might owe anything to her subtle expertise. He has never thought to ask about the peculiar-looking plants (calomel, aloes, black hellebore) that grow among the brambles at the end of the garden, or the bitter-smelling lotions and unguents which she sometimes leaves by accident on the kitchen table. He knows nothing about her craft, and asks nothing. So when Mrs Jakes insists, without a murmur of equivocation, that she delivered the shocking creature, and saw nothing amiss, he feels obliged to believe it.

Mrs Jakes applies herself again to the bedsheets. 'It'll want baptising,' she says.

'No doubt,' he answers, pensively stroking his side-whiskers.

'So you haven't seen it?'

'I have seen the crowd that waits upon it.'

'You will get a shock when you do.'

'I have been forewarned.'

'Forewarned is one thing,' says Mrs Jakes. 'Seeing with your own eyes is another.'

The chaplain snorts loudly. It seems to him sometimes that Mrs Jakes derives a grim satisfaction from his adversities; that she looks with sardonic amusement upon his efforts to teach the message of the Gospels to men who would rather roll up the pages of the Bible and smoke them. 'I had hoped,' he says peevishly, 'that your eyes would serve me as well.'

Mr Kidney is aware of the shameless tricks and evasions that convict women get up to. If Mrs Jakes had confessed to some doubts over the authenticity of the birth he would have been satisfied. He would not have wanted to know the details. He would have relied on Mrs Jakes's judgment, confident that God was not a party to it and that he, the colonial chaplain, was therefore excused from voicing an opinion. The fact that Mrs Jakes has vouched for the woman robs him of that excuse.

A brown snuffling thing appears at the window, which the Reverend Mr Kidney recognises as the nose of his horse, Nelson, rooting for something to eat among the stumps of his flowering annuals. The piebald gelding is perpetually breaking down the door of its stables and running amok in his flowerbeds.

Mrs Jakes scoops the sheet out of the water and wrings it between her warty hands. 'Captain Ainsworth,' she says, 'has returned from Kangaroo Island in the *Neptune* with three thousand seal skins and the same in kangaroos.'

The chaplain blows his nose and glances briefly at the contents. 'Indeed,' he mumbles, scrunching the handkerchief and putting it back in his pocket. 'Captain Ainsworth will leave nothing alive that has a pelt on it.' Then he shuffles away, head down, flat-footed, feeling the water squelch in his stockings.

~

On Thursday last the Largest conger Eel ever seen in this Colony was found in a Hole of Water on the Rocks near the Guard-house; its Length was 39 Inches and it weighed 12 Pounds. The Hole being some Distance from the Water's

Edge, it is supposed to have been dropped by a Seagull, as that Kind of Fish is principally the Maintenance of those Birds.

~

THERE ARE many things a seal pup cannot do. It cannot sit up at table. It cannot (or will not) eat chitterlings. It cannot kick a ball or fasten its own buttons or give any warning about the itch in its bowels. But what it can do is swim.

One morning, Sarah Dyer summons Ned from the wood-pile, where he's amusing himself tormenting lizards with a lighted stick, and tells him to take the creature for a dip.

The thing is now three weeks old and has a name, although its sex isn't any clearer. It is henceforth to be known as Arthur, in honour (says Mrs Dyer) of a handsome one-eyed gentleman she once met under the cliffs at Dover, who lent her his handkerchief and did not ask for it back.

Until now the pup has been content wallowing in an old bathtub. Mrs Dyer stitches up a pouch made from a pair of cotton trousers cut in half, with the leg tied off. The pup fits in snugly, with only its snout poking out. As soon as it gets a sniff of the sea it starts barking.

Ned is under strict orders not to let it stray from the rockpools. The pup seems happy enough floating on its back and splashing among the kelp, while Ned stands guard with a stick to keep the seagulls from pecking its eyes out.

A handful of drowsy fur seals are clinging to a rock not far from the shore. None of them takes any notice of the pup's cries—yoorh yoorh yoorh—echoing around the bay. Before long a rowboat comes around the headland: a small

navy cutter, heaving under a dozen casks of rum. The seals
spot it at once. They drop off the rock like burnt ticks. Ned
watches their heads pop up a hundred yards away, five silky
brown balls bobbing among the waves.

Ned kneels down to lift the pup out of the water. It wriggles through his hands, dives down to the bottom and comes
up again with a piece of kelp between its teeth. Yoorh yoorh
yoorh. 'Come back, Arthur,' shouts Ned. 'There's crabs an'
urchins and all sorts in there.' But the pup keeps swimming
around, slithering onto its back and splashing him with its
flippers.

Down on the beach there's a man standing up to his
chest in the water, his dark beard lapping against him like
seaweed. He hears Ned talking to the pup and looks round.
He doesn't wave. He just stands there, letting the surf break
over him, staring over his shoulder.

Ned picks up the trouser leg. He has seen strange
men down there before, old convicts with their wits gone,
wading out to sea as if they're planning to swim home to
England. Yoorh yoorh yoorh. 'Come on, Arthur,' whispers
Ned. 'It ain't safe here.' The pup glides to the edge of the
water, its black snout bristling with sea urchin quills which
Ned has to pull out one by one, shutting his ears to its
whimpering.

~

MRS JAKES'S business regularly draws her to the rust-streaked
gum tree opposite the shop of Messrs Lloyd and Lonsdale,
where satisfied mothers have sometimes been known to
post grateful acknowledgments of her services.

She never passes the tree without stopping to read the scraps of paper flapping in the wind, with their spidery pronouncements and bedraggled signatures. She is especially drawn to lists and inventories. It gives her great satisfaction to cast judgment on the latest shipments from London and Sydney. She nods at tea kettles and shakes her head at tortoiseshell combs. Or shakes her head at shoemakers' hemp and nods at ladies' calicoes. On some days she nods at black bonnets. On others she shakes her head. It depends on her mood.

Mrs Jakes is pondering the value of a winter consignment of grindstones and sealing wax, black and red ink powder, slates and pencils for sale at Mr Fryett's in Harrington Street, when it dawns on her that she is being watched.

A thin-lipped, sharp-nosed man is staring at her from across the street. He is wearing a tatty brown frockcoat and black triangular hat that complements his own angular features. His trousers are too short for him, exposing a strip of white flesh and several inches of grey stocking. One of his shoe buckles is missing. His collar is pulled up in an unsuccessful attempt to conceal a scar on his neck which seems to run from his Adam's apple to just behind his left ear, as if someone once tried to cut his throat.

Hobart Town, even in August, is full of itinerants, sealers and speculators, stowaways who have come to the colony by mistake, traders on their way to other settlements or just returned. They stay in the town for a week or a month, hanging around the docks, poring over notices, getting drunk, listening for news of some valuable plot of land which the surveyor has just marked out, half a day's ride to the north. Then they leave.

A cart rolls towards the harbour, slopping and sliding in the ruts. Mrs Jakes steps back to avoid the spray from the bullocks' hoofs. As the cart trundles past, a gust of wind flips the hat off the stranger's head, exposing a black furry skull. A moment later, he's gone.

~

Sale by Auction, by Mr LEWIS. At his Warehouse in Collins-street, on Saturday next, the 11th Instant, at Eleven O'clock in the Forenoon precisely, the following Articles; viz.—SIX Pipes of Cape-Madeira Wine; Four ditto of Muskadel ditto; Four Cases of stalk Raisins; Five ditto of picked ditto; One ditto of dried Apples; and Fourteen bags of Almonds. Prompt Payment required.

~

'AH, MR KIDNEY.'

The chaplain hesitates. 'You asked to see me?'

Mr Sculley looks bemused. The chaplain rummages in his breeches pocket for a crumpled scrap of paper. 'Your note, sir.'

Mr Sculley attaches his spectacles and reads the note. 'Yes, yes, of course. Forgive me. I had intended…never mind. You are here now. Come in.'

The Reverend Mr Kidney, suspecting that his good nature has been trespassed upon, stays where he is. The note (as far as he could decipher it) had implied that

Mr Sculley was in need of urgent spiritual counsel. Having imagined that its author was bedridden, the chaplain is irked to find him looking so healthy. 'I had expected to find you confined.'

'I am old, Mr Kidney, but far from incapacitated. Please come in.'

The chaplain enters and allows the door to be shut behind him. As he walks in he hears a loud banging noise, very close. He looks inquiringly at Mr Sculley, who either hasn't heard it, or pretends he hasn't. 'I take it this does not refer to a matter of conscience?'

Mr Sculley shakes his head. 'I believe my affairs are in order.'

'Then what...'

'I was hoping, sir...that is, it was my intention to consult your opinion...I wish to speak to you about the miraculous infant.'

The chaplain has half a mind to conclude the interview on the spot. But Mr Sculley, though he is an enthusiast, is no fool. The opportunity to hear the old gentleman's opinion of the birth, without soliciting it, inclines Mr Kidney to stay. He allows his expression to soften. 'I suppose you have examined it?'

'Examined it? Yes, sir, and weighed and measured it.' His eyelids flutter. 'I have it in every dimension, with some rough sketches in pencil and a whisker snipped from its chin.' He steers the chaplain into an armchair. 'It conforms, Mr Kidney, in every particular, to an infant seal or what is commonly called a pup.'

'I have heard that it is sadly deformed.'

'Not deformed, sir. Not deformed in the slightest. It is,

if I may say so, the perfect likeness of an infant seal in the rudest of health. There is not a doubt about it. The misfortunate woman, sir, has given birth to a seal pup.'

The chaplain looks around the room. There are numerous books lying open on the table, their mildewed pages covered with grotesque illustrations of women pregnant with dogs and griffins and two-headed babies and twins joined at the navel. Mr Sculley ferrets among them until he finds what he's after. 'Have you heard, Mr Kidney, of the sooterkin?'

'No.'

'It is a monstrous animal, with a hooked snout, fiery sparkling eyes, a long neck and the stump of a tail. Its fur is by some reports black and by others brown and it is universally remarked for its agility and fleetness of foot. At first sight of the world's light, it snarls and howls and runs about the chamber in search of a hole in which to hide.'

'A goblin.'

'You may call it a goblin if you like, sir, but the sooterkin was born in centuries past to several women in Holland, with distinguished surgeons and men of divinity in attendance. I have read their accounts.'

The chaplain hears a noise, like the sound of hammering, coming from the garden. 'And did this...sooterkin... have flippers, by any chance, and whiskers?'

'There is no mention of those appendages. In the opinion of those gentlemen who saw it, the sooterkin was not suited to water. I believe its closest resemblance was to a hare.'

'What is your point?'

'My point is this: we must not consider this nativity to

be entirely outside the possibility of nature. Women have given birth to much stranger things than seal pups.'

'And how, Mr Sculley, do you suppose they came by them?'

'By the imagination.'

A condescending smile passes over the chaplain's face. 'No doubt the philosophers support your contention.'

'Hippocrates and Plato have written concisely on the subject,' says Mr Sculley, glancing at the array of books on his table. 'As have Plutarch, Cicero and Saint Augustine.'

Mr Kidney's expression darkens at the last name. 'We have learnt, sir, not to trust the ancients in all things.'

'Indeed,' Mr Sculley continues, undaunted. 'Saint Thomas Aquinas has also vouched for the truth of it, and Martin Luther has accepted the doctrine.'

The chaplain heaves a sigh, intended to denote disdain, haughty amusement, Christian forbearance in the face of provocation. 'And how are we to suppose that the imagination is capable of spawning these monsters?'

'The imagination is a powerful...'

The chaplain interrupts by raising his hand. 'I am very thirsty. Might I ask...'

'I shall make tea at once.'

'Wine, sir, will suffice, if it is not an inconvenience.'

Mr Sculley fetches a bottle of claret and a glass. 'Medical literature, Mr Kidney, is full of cases of deformities caused by the excessive imagination of the mother. A pregnant woman will avoid the sight of a limbless beggar for fear that her child will inherit an identical injury. I have read of a Kentish woman whose husband was a poacher and caused her to give birth to a child with the neck and ears of a rabbit, and of a woman who saw a criminal broken on the wheel and then bore a child with limbs similarly fractured. A Welsh woman who watched the disembowelment of a lamb gave birth to a child whose viscera spilled from a cavity below its navel. A witness, Mr Kidney, was present in every case. Philippus Meurs, a canon of St Peter's in Rome, had a sister who was known to be ravenous for mussels and consequently gave birth to a child that had valves in its throat exactly like that shellfish. And a woman in Surrey…'

'Enough! This is mere market tittle-tattle. There is no authority for it.'

'Is the Bible sufficient authority?'

A long pause. 'There are no shellfish births in the Bible.'

'No,' says Mr Sculley. 'But Jacob placed stippled rods before his ewes and the ewes brought forth spotted lambs. What is this if not an experiment to prove the power of the imagination on the unborn child?'

The Reverend Mr Kidney reaches for the bottle. The thought that such an interpretation could be put upon Jacob's spotted lambs had not occurred to him. He is loath to acknowledge it now. Nevertheless, he is bound to accept that the authority of the Bible is not something to be picked up and set aside at will. If part of it is to be taken as literal truth, then all of it must be. He drains what is left in his glass. 'Did you ask the convict woman if she had dreamed of a seal?'

Mr Sculley beams with pleasure. 'I put that question to her, and she told me she had often dreamed of them, as her brother in Scotland is a sealer, and has spoken of join-ing her in Van Diemen's Land.'

'Then, sir, it appears your case is proved.'

Even the heaviest sarcasm is lost on Mr Sculley. The

idea that a man could say something and mean its opposite is one his empirical mind finds it impossible to grasp. He smiles graciously. 'I would not go so far, Mr Kidney. I wish merely to demonstrate that science does not scorn the unfamiliar. The very fact of a normal birth must presuppose the possibility of an abnormal one, just as a sound mind must carry within it the seeds of insanity.'

The chaplain has the uncomfortable feeling that the conversation is shifting under him. He refills his glass. 'I'm not with you, sir.'

'Science, Mr Kidney, is a tool with which to penetrate the unknown and decipher the unintelligible. It is the enemy of dogma, sir, as surely as indolence is the enemy of duty. Evidence is the key. A man cannot turn his back on evidence.'

The chaplain shrugs benevolently and allows his thoughts to drift out to sea while Mr Sculley expands on his theory. A brig is due in tomorrow or the next day from Sydney. Mr Kidney has high hopes that the cargo will include a twelve-gallon cask of madeira promised to him two months earlier by his brother-in-law, whose estate on the Hawkesbury River has grown even larger, and with no apparent effort on the part of its owner, while Mr Kidney's negligible wealth has inexorably contracted. The chaplain has never ceased to resent the injustice, but allows his jealousy to be mollified by sporadic gifts of liquor and shoes.

He feels a tap on his knee and looks up to see Mr Sculley waving his finger. 'You, of all people,' he says, 'will understand how near we are to barbarism.'

Mr Kidney gives vent to a solemn fart, which Mr Sculley mistakes for a grunt of assent.

'Indeed,' he continues, 'I did not imagine you could be ignorant of it, which is why I should value your opinion on my proposal.'

The chaplain drags his thoughts back from the Hawkesbury River. His brother-in-law sent him a sketch of the estate, with its grand house and elaborate gardens and what appeared to be a vineyard. 'Your proposal?'

'My idea is to found a settlement on the Isle of Bruny, based upon the strictest principles of physiognomy, whereby our existing society may be, as it were, quarantined, and may flourish without the taint or the temptation of crime.' He pauses to allow the chaplain to empty his glass. 'The population will, of course, need spiritual sustenance, which I had hoped you might be willing...'

The Reverend Mr Kidney gets unsteadily to his feet. He has listened long enough to the old man's waffling. Now that he has remembered the madeira he is anxious to arrange for its swift delivery. He thrusts out a plump paw which swallows up Mr Sculley's arthritic fingers. 'It is a very novel idea, sir. An extremely novel idea. I am glad to have heard it.'

'Then you will consider it?'

'I am, pardon me, considering it, sir. You may rest assured.' Another loud noise from the garden. Mr Kidney peers out of the window. 'What is that sound?'

Mr Sculley cocks his head to listen. The chaplain, suspecting some macabre experiment, hesitates before speaking again. It would do him no good to be complicit, even as an observer, in his host's scientific infatuations. Nevertheless, an intense curiosity, doused in claret, prevents him from leaving. He allows himself to be guided through the parlour, out of a narrow door and down a set of uneven steps into a garden enclosed by a high brick wall.

It could hardly be more different from his own intricate garden. Instead of the geometrical beds dug by convict labourers at his instruction, filled with carefully pruned bushes and precise rows of vegetables, Mr Sculley seems to have walled in a wilderness. There are trees swollen by staghorns and strangled by thick vines, flowering shrubs overrun with creepers, a handful of skeletal rose bushes choked by weeds. The walls themselves are encrusted with black and orange fungus.

The chaplain elbows past a clump of ferns. 'You are not fastidious in your gardening.'

'The vegetation suits me, Mr Kidney. I do not care to tame it.'

Mr Sculley leads him along a short path to a wooden crate, about the height of a man, with a door cut into it, and a small peephole, through which the chaplain spies an indignant kangaroo lying on a carpet of straw.

'It is a common kangaroo, is it not?'

As if in reply, the kangaroo launches a violent two-footed kick at the side of the crate, causing Mr Kidney to stagger backwards in alarm. This, he realises, is the noise he has been hearing.

'Common or not,' says Mr Sculley, helping the chaplain to his feet, 'it is without doubt a kangaroo.'

'Must I ask why you have confined it?'

Mr Sculley presses his own eye to the peephole. 'Did you see its pouch?'

'I saw that it had one. I could not see what was in it.'

'Eggs, sir. I have placed two goose eggs in the pouch.'

Mr Kidney stops brushing the litter from his breeches.

He stares at Mr Sculley as he would at a bishop lighting his pipe in the pulpit. The idea seems both mad and sacrilegious.

'It is an experiment, sir.'

'And what will it prove? That the kangaroo is cousin to the goose?'

Mr Sculley feels a rush of blood to his cheeks. 'You belittle science, sir.'

'No,' says the chaplain, pulling a vine out of his face. 'It is science that belittles you. If the Almighty had meant the kangaroo to carry eggs, He would have provided them. Your experiment will fail because it affronts God and nature. Your science is mere alchemy, sir. Good day.'

~

WHAT IS it like to be kissed by a seal pup? It's like nuzzling tripe. Or blowing your nose on a stinging nettle. Its mouth is a sump of fish and seaweed and rotten gums. Its teeth are brown and there are lice hopping in its whiskers. But the pup won't kiss William Dyer on account of his tobacco breath, which is even gamier that its own. And Sarah Dyer, having surrendered to such intimacies as a mother could hardly refuse her newborn, is reluctant to encourage any more. Which leaves Ned as the sole object of the creature's affections, and scarcely able to show his face without getting rasped and whiskered to death.

Wherever they go, the pair of them are stared at and gawped over, petted by ladies and jeered by beggars and sniffed by dogs and horses. Ned hardly knows which is worse, the hungry curs skipping after them on the beach or the rich old widows hounding them in Georges Square.

Since the pup was born the family has eaten nothing but pork chops, each as thick as a ship's oar, burnt to a cinder and floating in a puddle of fat. Sarah Dyer lets the bones pile up outside the back door as proof of their changed fortune. Ticket-of-leave men, all scabs and sores, poke their heads over the fence to stare at the midden, licking their lips, hoping the meat will grow back if they stare hard enough. At dusk Sarah shoos them away with a broom.

The pup brings in a steady stream of clipped pennies and battered sixpences, plus the occasional Dutch guilder and Spanish pistole from sailors too drunk to know what's in their pockets. But Sarah Dyer has grander plans in mind. She stares at her husband and says, 'I've a mind to put Arthur in a circus.'

William Dyer scrapes the fat to the edge of his plate and raises a spoonful to his lips. 'A circus, missus?'

'That's what I said.'

He opens his mouth wide and shovels the fat towards the swinging red bells of his tonsils. 'I never heard of a circus coming here.'

'That's because it hasn't.'

Dyer glances at Ned, as if he might be able to make sense of the conversation. He licks the back of the spoon. 'You've lost me, missus.'

'We must have our own circus,' says Sarah.

'Must we?' asks Dyer, staring at his reflection in the back of the spoon.

'Yes,' she says, snatching his plate away. 'We must.'

Dyer removes a twist of tobacco from his whiskers and lets it burn in the candle flame. The tobacco shrivels up without a sound. It is a great mystery to him how tobacco can burn so quietly in a flame, and yet so noisily in a pipe, where it spits and crackles like coals in a brazier. It strikes him that much of the pleasure a man gets from smoking a pipe comes from the agreeable noise it makes while burning, and that a silent pipe would be a miserable thing to suck on. This thought reminds him that his own tobacco pouch is empty and needs filling, which cannot be accomplished without a shilling from Mrs Dyer's purse. 'You're right exactly, missus,' he says. 'We must get ourselves a circus.'

~

The PUBLIK is hereby informed that our HUMAN PUP, sent to us by the GRACE of GOD, can be seen at his TRICKS by interested Persons at 2 each Afternoon (the Lords day ixepted) or by privit Arangment with the OWNER, at very modest Cost.

~

SARAH DYER orders the following, as the bare minimum needed to attract a paying audience of soldiers, shopkeepers, jobless ticket-of-leave men, clerks with nothing to do, traders with nothing to sell, truant servants, lost sailors and idle harbourmen:

Six wooden chairs, hired from Mr Biggins the undertaker at sixpence a week each;
Six cushions, ditto, a penny each;
Three benches, built by Mr Stanley the wheelwright, a shilling each;

One cotton sheet from Messrs Lloyd and Lonsdale,
threepence;

One bonnet, ditto, tuppence;

One ship's pulley, origin unknown, fourpence;

One skittle, found by Ned near the bond store;

One ball, hand-sewn from a pig's bladder by Mrs Pleat,
tuppence.

At sixpence a head for the chairs, and tuppence for the
benches, Sarah Dyer expects to make a pound a week—a
sprightly income that will have them living in bricks and
mortar before next winter. She has Mr Bent print up a few
dozen handbills and stations Ned by the gate to collar
passers-by, while William Dyer lurches up and down the
street, listening to his pipe, and consulting the tin watch he
bought from a pickpocket for half a crown.

Hobart Town isn't exactly abuzz with entertainment.
Apart from the chaplain's Sunday sermon, and the
regimental band, and Mrs Sweetwater's string quartet
(minus the cello, which sank off Tenerife), it comes down
to two choices: reading for the quality and ratting for the
rest. A circus, even if it's only Ned and the pup tossing a
skittle between them, is bound to pull them in, and does.

Sarah Dyer stands by the door relieving the punters of
their money, while Ned and the pup crouch behind the
sheet having a last run-through. At exactly five minutes to
two by his watch, William Dyer removes the pipe from his
mouth and taps it briskly against his heel. A group of
Wesleyans are gathered outside, clutching their Bibles, loath
to enter the house but eager to catch a glimpse from where
they stand. Others loiter by the gate, hoping to be called
in at the last minute to make up the numbers. Dyer hitches

up his pants and shoulders his way imperiously through the rabble.

The audience is inside, fifteen of them jostling for room on the benches, six drunk, two hungover, shouting at Mrs Dyer to get on with it before they demand their money back. Most are assigned servants and harbourmen. Nothing here smarter than a Russian furrier, but never mind, thinks Sarah, fluffing out her skirts, tuppence is tuppence.

William Dyer attempts a smile to his wife—which goes unreciprocated—as she shuts out the Wesleyans. He nods to sundry acquaintances on the benches, delivers an unscripted bow to the Russian, winks at one of the harbourmen.

Then up goes the sheet, hoisted aloft on the ship's pulley, scaring the life out of the pup, which tries to burrow up Ned's trouser leg. Their first applause of the afternoon, and they haven't even started. Dyer claps loudly: 'Bravo, Arthur, old son!' His wife shoots a dark look at the boy as she rubs the filth off a halfpenny piece.

At last Ned coaxes the pup out of his trousers. He picks up the bladder and bounces it from hand to hand. 'Catch, Arthur!' The pup watches it sail across the room and land in the Russian's lap. Rowdy cries from the English sailors. Slanders on the name of the dead empress.

'Give the boy his bladder back!'

'Bugger off back to Muscovy!'

Sarah Dyer, the impresario, edges closer to the front, where she can keep an eye on troublemakers. 'The spoons!' she hisses.

Another little trick they've been working on: Ned juggles a pair of spoons while the pup croaks and claps its flippers.

But someone has stolen the spoons. Ned takes a bow anyway, but the pup doesn't move. It just stares at him, head tilted, waiting for a fish.

Sarah Dyer requests the return of the spoons, which cost her a penny each from a chandler's shop in Collins Street. A drunken ticket-of-leave man threatens to pick the Russian up by his ankles and shake him until the spoons fall out. Two sailors roll up their sleeves to air their tattoos. Ned and the pup stare at each other, wondering what to do next, as one of the harbourmen falls over a chair.

All of a sudden the pup starts mewling. It's a queer, plangent noise, like a barrel organ played underwater, interrupted every so often by a raucous bark. But if you listen hard enough you can hear a tune, a muffled melody that might be a verse from one of Mr Wesley's hymns, cut short by a bark, and then another tune that sounds just like a sea shanty. William Dyer looks at his wife. Sarah Dyer looks at Ned. They all stare at the pup, croaking out a few bars of a sailor's hornpipe and keeping time with its flipper.

Before long, the sailors join in. Someone brings out a penny whistle. The harbourmen start clapping. Even the Russian stretches his creased face into a smile.

While the Wesleyans press their foreheads to the window, Mrs Dyer stoops for a bucket to receive any spontaneous tributes that might be forthcoming. She shuffles among the benches, offering her hand to the harbourmen, brushing their knees with her skirts. Thank you, thank you, too kind sir, ain't they a lovely pair, I taught 'em everything but I never seen 'em do it so well.

She collects three shillings and ninepence, a silver rouble from the Russian, two musket balls and half a dozen buttons.

As William Dyer gazes at the coins, Ned falls on the pup and tickles its throat and blows its whiskers and plays hide-and-seek with a herring, until the pup wriggles out of his grasp and takes refuge in its cot.

~

We are ashamed to report that the Bush-rangers, who lately robbed Mr STOCKER at Bagdad, have since removed to Pitt-Water, where they committed an Outrage on the Property of Colonel DAVEY, once Lieutenant-Governor of this Colony. The Bandits were MICHAEL BRODIE, DANIEL SEPTON and JAMES WATTS, with some others who did not show their Faces. Colonel DAVEY was absent at the Time of the Attack, or we are assured the Miscreants would already be regretting their Boldness in Gaol. The Bandits burnt two Haystacks and helped themselves to the Contents of Col DAVEY's Cellar. A Servant who attempted to thwart them was beaten and a Female of the House rudely handled by such Ruffians as would flee from the Presence of a robust Constable, if one could be found.

~

AUGUST SPLASHES on. Colonel Tom Davey whips his bloated carcass into the field, determined to ride down the bushrangers who set fire to his haystacks. With his scarlet tunic straining across his belly he looks like a wineskin about

to burst. You can hear his churning insides twenty feet away.
He gallops out of Pitt Water with a dozen flatfooted marines
stumbling in his wake.

They spend a day sheltering from the rain in one of
Edward Lord's stock sheds, while the bushrangers keep an
eye on them from their lookouts on the hills. The bandits
are in no hurry to move on. They have a couple of
Constable Murphy's best ewes tied up in the woods, and as
much grog as they can hold. And a handy network of convict
shepherds and stockmen to watch their backs and keep them
in powder and tobacco.

They burn down the police magistrate's barn in Pitt
Water, drive a hundred of Mr Lord's bullocks into a swamp
and hijack a merchant's cart in Black Snake. Then they
split up. Half head north to steal a boat from the garrison
at Port Dalrymple, board a trading brig in the straits and
sail to South America. Brodie, Septon and Watts stay behind
to raid the farms along the Fat Doe River.

The bandits have hideouts in Pitt Water and Clarence
Plains, in the hills above the Jordan River and the marshes
near Jericho and the woods around Jerusalem. Supplies
stashed all over the island. Two casks of salt beef and
half a dozen pistols in a cave on Cocked Hat Hill; dry
powder and shot in a shepherd's hut on the Styx River;
muskets wrapped in oilcloth in a hollow tree near
Blackman's Bay.

Three of them turn up at the Barley Mow Inn in Black
Snake, ten miles from Hobart Town, their horses newly
shod and hat ribbons flying from their saddles. The constable is out of town. Someone has had a friendly word in his
ear and he won't be back before dark.

They're wearing matching purple neckerchiefs and fancy Irish linen shirts, with muskets over their shoulders and pistols stuffed in their belts. They have a packhorse laden with shiny pots and pans and copper kettles—just the thing for rendering down beef suet.

The one in the seal-skin jacket is Michael Brodie, a big freckled Yorkshireman with red eyebrows that meet over his pug nose. Septon and Watts are shorter, stockier, with mean grins hidden in their bird's-nest beards. They put their pistols on the bar and ask for a shave. It's been two months since they saw a razor.

The trembling barber sets up his chair on the verandah. His tools aren't the flashest: rusty scissors, a broken shaving mirror, something in a green bottle that would singe the hairs in your nostrils. He has read the government posters, knows the seal-skin jacket, recognises each member of the gang from his description. One slip of the cut-throat razor could earn him a hundred guineas, but he wouldn't live to claim it.

The locals drift out to watch. The audience is mostly convict shepherds, stock-keepers, hired men, more likely to tip the bandits off than inform on them. They keep their distance all the same.

The publican sends out three mugs of ale, compliments of the house, while the barber lathers up. The best show in town is happening on his doorstep. A captive audience, happy to show its approval at the tap.

When the show is over, there's a pile of whiskers three inches deep around the chair. The sheet looks like a butcher's apron. The bandits strut about admiring themselves in the mirror, blood oozing into their neckerchiefs, their sun-starved chins as white as beef gristle.

'And what were you before you took up barbering?' asks Septon. 'A slaughterman?'

The crowd laughs. The barber smiles weakly and stares down at the floor. Michael Brodie tightens his trouser belt so the pistol won't fall out. 'What's the damage?'

The barber in an agony of indecision, a lump like an iron ball in his stomach, wipes away the blood with a wet flannel. 'It was my p-pleasure, gentlemen.'

Laughter. Two gold coins spin through the air, burying themselves in the mound of whiskers. 'Keep the blade steady next time, else we shan't be so generous.'

Three miles away, in Herdsman's Cove, the gang runs into a constable having a rotten tooth pulled by a quack. They've met the constable before. He does a bit of horse-dealing on the side. They find a set of leg irons hanging from his saddle, and a stockwhip, and a crumpled poster with a poor likeness of Michael Brodie. The quack recognises the bandits and slips away without a sound. The constable has his head back, eyes shut, mouth gaping, waiting for the tooth to be ripped out of his gums. Suddenly there's a musket barrel stuck halfway down his throat. Open wide. They knock out his front teeth with a pistol butt and hang them in a handkerchief around his neck, then leave him tied to a cartwheel with the poster stuffed in his mouth.

Colonel Davey rides into Black Snake to be told the bushrangers have been and gone. No complaints from the marines, who are happy to let them go. They push on to Herdsman's Cove and find the constable tied to his cartwheel, as stiff as a corpse but still breathing. The soldiers cut him down but the constable won't talk. Davey returns to Hobart Town with a bloody barber's sheet and three shaved beards in a sack, two unmarked heifers which he dragged out of a bog and a copper kedgeree pot worth five guineas.

~

NOTICE—The PUP will sing at 2 each afternoon. Tickets 1 Shilling. Please be promt. Large ordience ixpected.

~

IF THERE is one thing smarter than a seal pup, it's an octopus. An octopus can slip between the bars of a lobster pot when the gate is down and pick the lobster clean. It can pull the bung out of a cask of pickled sprats, steal the sprats and replace the bung if it wants to. It can tie a porpoise up in knots, pull down a muttonbird and swallow a sea urchin whole.

Ned has heard it said that if you cut one tentacle off an octopus, two more will grow in its place, which is why (says Ned) an octopus, when it is hauled up in the nets by mistake, must be bludgeoned with an oar or else put back unharmed.

He takes the pup down to the beach and draws a huge octopus in the sand, with more tentacles than were ever seen on a real one. But the pup just looks at the squiggly lines and barks as the tide washes them away.

A week later there is a fierce storm. By morning the beach at Sullivan's Cove is littered with seaweed and driftwood and the bodies of fish tossed ashore by the waves. The pup dives into its favourite rockpool, only this time it doesn't come up.

Ned waits and waits. He claps his hands and whistles.

He bends down and starts raking at the kelp. Then he sees it: an old warty octopus with a blackish-purple body as big as a sheep's udder and sly beady eyes, with the pup trussed up in its tentacles.

Ned grabs a stick and pokes one of its eyeballs. A tentacle flies out and tries to snatch away the stick. Ned pokes the other eyeball. The octopus spins around, dragging the pup under a ledge. It stays there, pressed like a barnacle against the rock, while Ned prods and stabs it with his stick, too scared to put his arm in the water.

Just when it seems the pup is doomed, a cry goes up— 'Arthur!'—and Sarah Dyer comes charging down the beach, skirts billowing around her thighs and piece of driftwood in her hand, with which she batters the octopus senseless, and not a moment too soon.

~

SPRING IS coming. The mud has begun to stiffen in the wind. The whey-faced clerks in the bond store come out at lunchtime, remove their hats, loosen their collars, and let the sun warm their brains. Even James McCluskey, the half-blind ship's agent, has been observed emerging from his bothy and sniffing the fragrant breeze like a mole.

The chaplain's stone cottage stinks of paint and turpentine, the front door and shutters freshly daubed in black as a pious rebuke to the swaggering brick mansions on both sides. The acrid, nose-puckering smells creep from room to room, mixing with the odour of stale tobacco smoke and rosewater wafting from an open bottle on Mr Kidney's writing desk.

The chaplain is considering a postscript to a letter which has been sitting for several weeks, unfinished, in a locked box on the top shelf of his bookcase. The letter is addressed to the Reverend Mr Samuel Marsden, Bishop of Sydney, and contains Mr Kidney's thoughts on the birth and subsequent prospering of the seal pup.

Mr Kidney has still not been able to bring himself to favour the parents with a visit, but has had the opportunity to view the creature numerous times in the care of the boy. Having listened to Mrs Jakes's testimony, and considered Mr Sculley's appeals to nature, and pored over the more temperate books of the Old Testament, he has manoeuvred himself into a state of sulky equivocation. That the infant represents an aberration is undeniable. That God has sanctioned it is, at the very least, open to question. Whether it is a seal pup or a sooterkin or some other thing without a name seems to make little difference. And whether science will unravel the mystery, or faith, is something upon which the chaplain is unwilling to speculate.

~

Hobart Town
Van Diemen's Land

Sir,

I take the liberty to address you in the belief that word will have reached you (from what source I will not venture to presume) concerning the birth of a creature that does not conform in all respects to those already witnessed in this colony. Those discrepancies have led vicious minds to encourage distasteful speculation regarding the manner of its conception. I need hardly add that the standard of medical practice in Hobart Town is not such as to inspire confidence in its ability to distinguish the normal from the abnormal, or to discriminate among those subtle shades of human variation which are the truest proof of God's purpose in creating Mankind.

The common support cleaves to the Mother, although scepticism holds sway among those pleased to consider themselves educated. My inclination is to treat with caution such wild rumours and allegations as have already been fanned into life and to guard my opinions until unequivocal evidence can be procured that will decide the question in the positive or the negative. I do not consider myself qualified to adjudicate on that which pits Instinct against Knowledge, and Science against the Bible, yet I venture to suggest that it is in the Incomprehensible, and not the Obvious, that we most powerfully discern the scope and tendency of the Creator's plan.

I could append to this letter several pages of speculation, but speculation is not proof, and we cannot presume on Human Intellect to illuminate what God has chosen, for the time being, to obscure. That He is capable of any Miracle is beyond our capacity to doubt. It is possible that the Almighty has cultivated this Mystery in order to exercise our minds in searching after the divine and valuable Truths concealed within it.

Were you to honour this island with a visit, I believe you would better appreciate its Strangeness, and the peculiar Distress of its citizens. Such a visit would perhaps instil in you an understanding of the macabre events which continue to be visited upon us and which, like stones in a still pond, cast their reverberations far beyond our own treacherous shores.

We are a colony beset with Monstrosity, as much in the commission of sin as in the punishing of it, and so inured to the Unnatural that the Natural itself seems wondrous and terrible. I enclose for your contemplation the body of a creature discovered not a mile from where I sit, which has the snout and webbed feet of a Duck engrafted on the velvet body of a Quadruped, and is in consequence of its eccentric configuration referred to as a Duck-billed Mole, although it might as easily be called a Goose-rat, or Fish-scorpion, as it both lays Eggs and gives Suck to its young, yet it spends the greater part of its existence beneath the water and carries a poisonous Sting on its feet. No man has seen the creature hatched, far less conceived, and yet, as you can see for yourself, it exists.

I hope, sir, this Letter finds you in good Health as, for the time being, it leaves me.

Obediently yours,
Thos. Kidney

~

WILLIAM DYER walks in and slaps a parcel of beef shins down on the table. A fretful look on his face announces that he has been thinking, or more likely talking to someone else who has been thinking, and the other man's thoughts have rubbed off on him, and now they're bothering him.

Sarah Dyer scowls at the bloody package and prods it with the end of her switch broom. She looks at Ned and scowls at her husband, and looks at her husband and scowls at Ned, as though the beef shins were a conspiracy between them. She tells Ned to go outside and fetch a pot of water for boiling.

Dyer thumbs tobacco into his pipe and sets fire to it with a taper while Sarah carries on sweeping. She sweeps the dust into a pile and observes tartly that, for all its airs and graces, it is no better than the dust she used to sweep before they came into money.

Dyer hitches up his leather waistcoat and holds his backside so close to the fire that soon he is smoking from both ends. 'How old is Arthur?' he asks. 'More or less.'

'Never mind more or less. He is two months and a day.'

'And is the lad ahead of his age or behind it?'

'He is neither.'

Dyer removes the pipe from his mouth and allows the smoke to dribble out of him. 'I've been talking, missus, to a gentleman that is familiar with the case.'

'And what case is that, husband?'

'I mean Arthur.'

'What of it?'

'The gentleman is of the opinion…'

'Was this gentleman, by any chance, acquainted with the taps of the Bird-in-Hand?'

Dyer scowls and steps away from the fire. 'The gentleman, missus, was pleased to let me have his private opinion on the matter, which he got of another gentleman, a friend of his, that married a Dutchwoman and swore that Arthur had the look of a sooterkin.'

She eyes him suspiciously. 'And what's one of them when it's at home?'

'It's a saucy creature is what it is, that comes on a woman when she's expectin', and has queer habits and a tail and is written about by parsons.'

'I hope you ain't been flapping that big tongue of yours,' says Sarah. 'I've got enough worries as it is.'

Dyer puts the pipe back in his mouth and pats his pockets for tobacco. He sidles over to the table, where he can keep an eye on the beef shins. 'What worries?' he asks.

'Tell him, boy.'

'There's a captain tried to buy Arthur for five guineas, and Mam wouldn't let him, and said she'd let him have the poker if she caught him skulking.'

'What captain?'

'Never mind what captain,' says Sarah. 'I didn't ask his name.'

He ponders the matter for a minute or two. 'Tell him it ain't enough.'

'I'll do nothing of the sort. I told him what I had to say and that's the end of it. Arthur ain't for sale.'

A long pause follows, during which William Dyer inserts and removes the pipe at least a dozen times before noticing that it has gone out. He furrows his brow and scratches his chin and rolls his eyes like a man who can't find his spectacles because they're sitting on his nose. He wonders how long it would take a man (himself, say) to smoke his way through five guineas' worth of tobacco, or to drink his way through five guineas' worth of rum. He wonders how it would feel to be measured up for a pair of five-guinea breeches. Or to screw a five-guinea hat on his head. It seems to him that five guineas is not an amount to be taken up or given away without careful thought, and that such thoughts are best entertained over a pot of mulled ale. He brushes some ash off his sleeve. 'Quite right, missus,' he says.

~

MR KIDNEY is not fond of his horse. And Nelson, being a sensitive creature, is not fond of him. They cohabit on the chaplain's third of an acre in a state of mutual distrust. The fact that horse and chaplain are estranged is mainly the fault of Mr Kidney, who has grown too fat for his saddle, and is thus a far greater burden than the animal bargained for in the early, amicable days of their partnership. Meanwhile the standard of its own keep has declined. The animal has to make do with poorer hay, and less of it. There are also grounds for complaint in the matter of grooming. If it is not reading too much into the mind of a quadruped, Mr Kidney's piebald gelding could be said to nurse a number of grievances, any one of which might explain its refractory behaviour. The chaplain attributes it to a vicious temperament. There is, in truth, a good deal of Mr Kidney in his horse, and a good deal of his horse in him. They do their best to avoid each other but have learned to accept that this is not always possible.

If a journey needs making and Mr Kidney cannot wheedle his way into the lieutenant-governor's barouche, he tries to borrow Mr Waddy's dog cart, although the springs are worn and the axle is bent and the wheel rims need fixing. He would be sitting in it now, squeezed into its scuffed leather seat on his way to visit a dying farmer in York Plains, if Mr Waddy had not chosen this morning to count his cattle.

The chaplain was informed of this (brusquely, with a smirk) by Mrs Waddy, who is a Wesleyan, and disapproves of clergymen travelling in dog carts. If it was up to Mrs Waddy, the chaplain would tour his parish on foot, in sandals and sackcloth.

Mr Waddy's is not the only dog cart in Hobart Town. There are other dog carts, in worse states of repair, but their owners are not in the habit of lending them, at least not to the chaplain, and not for travelling forty miles to York Plains over roads that barely deserve the name. So Mr Kidney, in accordance with his pastoral vows, has this morning been obliged to saddle his beast for a visit that may yet turn out to be futile.

The farmer, William Wheeler, took ill on the first day of September; it is now the seventeenth. In the absence of any reliable medical opinion, there is no guessing the extremity of his condition. Fevers, once they have taken hold, have a habit of racing to a morbid conclusion. It would not be the first time the chaplain had arrived too late to usher a dying man into heaven.

Had a neighbour's son not ridden the forty miles alone, and begged him to make the journey, Mr Kidney might have found pressing reasons for staying at home. But the chaplain, whatever his own disappointments, is not immune to the notion of sacrifice. He is not an uncaring man, though most of his concern is reserved for himself. And three days of auspiciously fine weather—with the prospect of more ahead—have convinced him that he should, after all, undertake the mission, despite Mrs Sweetwater's strenuous objections.

Perhaps it has not entirely slipped his mind that William

Wheeler is in possession of an IOU written by himself for the sum of twenty guineas, to cover the purchase of six heifers. Why the chaplain should ever have wanted to buy six heifers, and what he intended to do with his purchase, are questions Mr Kidney would now find it difficult to answer. But during the long winter of 1812 there was money to be made from speculating in beef, and he was persuaded to engage in it, though not with his own capital. His investment proved disastrous. His heifers did not live long enough to be butchered and welcomed into the commissariat meat store but were driven off by bushrangers while grazing among Mr Lord's herd beside the Shannon River.

It might have occurred to the chaplain that the question of an outstanding IOU could arise in the course of a dying man's reflections and that the aforesaid IOU might be magnanimously returned, or torn up in his presence, or discounted by some charitable percentage.

Such thoughts might have influenced Mr Kidney's decision, or they might not. In any case, he has made up his mind to go and is now trotting along Elizabeth Street at half past seven on a Monday morning with a view to catching the second ferry of the day, riding solidly until lunchtime, and reaching his destination soon after three o'clock. The neighbour's boy, having fallen sick from his efforts, has been left behind to suffer one of Mrs Jakes's purgatives.

The chaplain is carrying with him a leather satchel containing his Bible, prayer book and hymnal. He has a rough map drawn by a sergeant in the surveyor's detachment, as well as a meagre picnic lunch (salt pork, biscuits, walnuts, a wrinkled apple) packed by Mrs Jakes the night before.

In case of bad weather on the return journey, he has brought a heavy brown oilskin, which Mrs Jakes has managed to attach to his saddle by means of a leather strap. The last and most impressive item of equipment is a hand-tooled Belgian fowling piece, one of a pair given to him by Lord Spencer, loaded with birdshot. The gun is slung over his shoulder in a manner that suggests its primary purpose is display.

Mr Kidney has lived in the colony long enough to understand the arbitrariness of its dangers. A man could ride to Pitt Water after dark in perfect safety, and yet be set upon in broad daylight within sight of the barracks gate. The presence of a constable is no guarantee of protection, since most are in cahoots with the bandits, and the rest have learned to turn a blind eye.

The columns of the *Hobart Town Gazette* are full of menace: cold-blooded bushrangers, lawless savages, scavenging beasts that live in the carcasses of dead cattle. Mrs Jakes insists on reading the most lurid narratives aloud over breakfast. But these have not undermined a belief in his own immunity that amounts sometimes to recklessness, sustained by a truculent if misguided sense of his own authority.

Blacks are the least of his fears. Once or twice a year, they appear without warning in his garden. They come before dawn and are there when he wakes up: children, sinewy old men with milky cataracts, mothers with infants in fur bundles. He peers out of his bedroom window and sees them huddled in the middle of the lawn, waiting for him to come out. They leave no footprints but seem to have floated in like the mist. They present him with bags of berries, fresh mackerel, young wallabies lashed with vines. He gives them Bibles and painted china dolls and English pears that make them sick. The women and children finger his clothes, poking his belly with their long fingers. The old men stand there grinning, long spears gripped between their toes. He lets them stroke his whiskers and peer through his spectacles. He reports these placid encounters to the Bishop of Calcutta, enclosing simple artefacts that might be of interest.

He knows there are others, savages with clay in their hair and scars gouged deep into their chests, who spear cattle and burn farms. The cattle are found with their buttocks missing, the carcasses covered with branches. It would never occur to Mr Kidney that the blacks who gather stoically on his lawn might be the same as the renegades who spear cattle; he would be horrified to learn that some of the men hunted down by farmers and convict stockmen have been found with the limbs of china dolls strung around their necks.

It is his opinion that peaceful blacks outnumber the rest. He believes the Gospels, even in the crude form in which he is obliged to impart them, are able to touch the most barbarous soul, and that some primitive Christian understanding has already begun to take root among the native population. He deplores the rumours that sometimes reach his ears of exterminations carried out in the name of pacification, of minor offences provoking merciless retribution. He believes the blacks have no cause to harm him, and won't.

As for bushrangers, his chief protection is that he has nothing worth stealing except his horse.

Mr Kidney passes a stand of gum trees which has so far escaped the timbercutters' saws, and trots along the broad muddy path that leads to the ferry crossing. The River Derwent is down several feet since the rains. Brown waves are clawing lazily at its banks. He turns his horse towards the short timber wharf and manages to dismount without injuring himself. The ferryman accepts a grunt in lieu of a tip and assists Mr Kidney in shoving his horse onto the ferry.

As the chaplain steps aboard, he glances gingerly at the other passengers: a sandy-haired trader taking tobacco and grog to the farmers along the Clyde River and a hungry-looking settler and his goat. Both men avoid his gaze. It is less than a month since seven men drowned when the ferry capsized in midstream. The bodies of two more were never found. The ferryman himself, a short bullet-headed Cornishman, was the only survivor. The chaplain buried the victims side by side in the cemetery behind the church.

The ferry is about to cast off when a fourth passenger arrives—a well-dressed man whose dark skin and louche looks mark him out at once in the chaplain's mind as a foreigner. This gentleman hesitates before entrusting his heel to the gangplank, as if weighing up the vessel's seaworthiness. He notes the shattered timber railing on the port side and the rudder shaft bound with rope. He presses the point of his stick between the freshly tarred planks. Finally he steps aboard.

The Reverend Mr Kidney fingers the brim of his hat and says in a hopeful voice, 'A sound vessel, sir?' The foreign gentleman looks at him quizzically without answering.

The ferryman waits until he is certain nobody else is

coming, then pushes off, glaring at each passenger in turn, as if they are to blame for the ferry being only half full.

As the flat, square-fronted vessel noses towards the middle of the river, the hawsers begin to stretch. The stern slews downstream and the goat scampers forward and the chaplain has to jerk the reins to stop his horse doing likewise. The ferryman mumbles to himself, and the sandy-haired trader, who has the most (in pounds sterling) to lose, mutters something to the foreign gentleman, who doesn't reply.

There are two men waiting on the opposite bank with a pair of kangaroo dogs and what looks like a bundle of skins, bound with ropes. Each has a musket slung over his shoulder. One is sitting on the bundle, scratching himself and idly tossing stones into the river. The other is squatting on his haunches, blowing clouds of smoke from a long clay pipe.

The landing has undergone some alterations since Mr Kidney's last crossing. A number of stout wooden poles have been driven into the mud beside the jetty, apparently to stop it breaking free and floating downstream. From one of these poles a small dinghy fidgets in the current. A small structure, like a dovecote, is taking shape nearby. The beginnings of a roof have been erected over part of the jetty, although the major part is entirely exposed. There is more timber piled on the bank, in anticipation of further improvements.

The chaplain's horse stamps impatiently as the ferry drifts towards the bank, alarming the goat, which tries to throw itself overboard. 'Keep 'im quiet,' growls the settler, 'before we all get drownded.'

Mr Kidney frowns at the irascible gelding, which snorts and shoulders him against the railing.

It crosses the chaplain's mind to delay setting off, so as not to betray his intentions to the two men on the bank, whose studied carelessness now seems distinctly sinister. It would be no great inconvenience to wait half an hour, or to ride away from the road before rejoining it a mile or two further on. The land on both sides of the river is dotted with farms linked by paths and muddy cattle tracks, most of which Mr Kidney has ridden along at some time or another.

The finer details of his plan (a settler's wife insisting he stop for lunch, sheep's liver sizzling in his honour, brandy pressed on him for the journey) are beginning to form when the ferry bumps against the timber jetty and the ferryman clambers ashore to secure it against the current.

Before the chaplain can catch his breath, he's being pulled by his horse down the gangplank and up the steep muddy slope that will soon turn into the road to Port Dalrymple. He glances again at the trappers, who look less menacing up close than they had from a distance. One of them he half recognises. The other offers a grin that might, with some effort, be interpreted as a smile. Neither makes any show of moving until the last passenger has disembarked. The ferryman appears to know them both and waves them aboard for the return trip.

The chaplain takes a swig of brandy from his silver flask and heaves himself into the saddle. A fat drop of rain tumbles out of a sky that moments ago had been cloudless, and splashes inauspiciously on his nose.

~

WHILE THE Reverend Mr Kidney is scrambling up the bank, a slick Yankee schooner, the *Seagull*, is dropping anchor in

Sullivan's Cove. It bobs in the lee of Hunter's Island, moaning and straining, keeping its republican distance from the English brigs and naval cutters.

The *Seagull* has spent the night among the whalers in Storm Bay and sloped into the harbour at dawn. There are telescopes trained on it from the Customs House, and clerks ready to poke their inky fingers into its cargo. Already an officer has been ashore and posted notices outside the inns, looking for two men to replace the pair swept overboard off the Cape.

A small group of convicts is standing on the wharf, toasting their hands over a brazier. Two marines, a gnarled corporal and a young private, are lounging against a wall. Further along the wharf, other marines are slouched over their muskets, making sure nothing is taken off the *Seagull* before the customs men get aboard. Americans are smugglers and revolutionaries, and Lieutenant-Governor Sorell won't have subversive liquor washing around the streets of Hobart Town.

There's a surgeon aboard, moderately famous around the state of Massachusetts, especially among the rich Boston squires and their wives.

At least the man calls himself a surgeon, is introduced as such by the captain, and carries a black leather hold-all with a selection of shiny instruments—saws, scissors, probes, callipers—that might plausibly belong to a surgeon, or a horse doctor. Also a patented machine for manufacturing pills, and another machine with a polished steel pincer for extracting musket balls from wounded soldiers.

The surgeon's name is Banes, Dr Benjamin Banes of Harvard. A teetotaller. Forty-four years old with a wife and a host of female admirers enchanted by the problems of removing a musket ball from a dying marine without the use of a scalpel. A slim dapper lavender-scented gentleman with gold-rimmed spectacles and backers in several cities who have invested upwards of a thousand dollars each for the privilege of being associated with his machines.

The *Seagull* has put in to Hobart Town en route for Port Jackson, where Dr Benjamin Banes has high hopes of demonstrating his inventions (and an ingenious design for a steam-driven stomach pump) to Governor Macquarie. The ship's captain has some hopes of picking up a consignment of skins cheap enough to make the detour worthwhile, and selling them in Sydney.

The settlement reminds Banes of the more squalid parts of Boston, near the docks, where he occasionally goes looking for sailors willing to have their stomachs mechanically siphoned for a dollar.

The chances of meeting anyone worth meeting in Hobart Town had struck him as too remote to justify the trouble of going ashore. Banes would have been content to stay in his cabin had Boxer, the bosun's mate, not blurted out what he'd heard about a woman giving birth to a seal pup.

It is not the first time Banes has heard such stories. Boston whores are always giving birth to creatures that are not quite human, mulatto infants with missing toes or cleft jaws or arms twisted behind their backs. These and other similarly gruesome abortions have been delivered to him in deference to his reputation as an inventor, as if such unsightly modifications to the human blueprint might be considered suitable material for the patent office.

A seal pup is a different matter. A pup, furthermore, that is reputed to hold a tune and perform tolerably well with a skittle. Banes has never heard of a woman giving birth to a seal pup, or any other marine creature for that matter. A musical seal pup is worth an hour ashore, even in such a wretched place as this.

Boxer rows him to a small private jetty far enough from the loading wharves not to attract attention. Banes averts his gaze from a dead dog lying on its back in the street, its ribs crushed by a cartwheel. Another dog sidles up to it, sees Banes and Boxer, and skulks away into the bushes.

The two men trudge up the hill, wading like flamingoes between the piles of bullock shit, until they see the crowd ahead of them, a dozen or so, standing outside a weather-board shack. Scrofulous convicts and wild-haired women in mud-streaked aprons turn to stare at Banes in his satin-collared coat and yellow stockings. A crippled child buries its face in its mother's skirts.

'You're certain this is the place, Mister Boxer?'

Boxer nods, keeping his hand on the pistol pushed into his pants.

The smell of pork fat seeps through the walls. While applying a dab of lavender water to his handkerchief, Banes casts his eye over a handbill nailed to the front door. Observing that the door is ajar, he invites Boxer to push it open.

Sarah Dyer looks up from the ledger in which she and Ned are admiring the weekend's takings. 'My apologies, sir. The recital is not for hours yet. Come back later if it suits you, or tomorrow if you'd rather.'

Banes removes his hat and enters the room, stepping over a wooden skittle and a bowl of sprats, pausing to examine a hand-sewn pig's bladder and weighing up the likely purpose of various other pieces of theatrical apparatus. Finally his gaze falls on the seal pup, or at least one of its flippers, poking out of a mound of blankets in the corner of the room. 'Are you the owner of this, er, melodious individual?'

'I'm the mother, sir, if that's what you mean.' Sarah Dyer looks admiringly at the visitor's velvet frockcoat, unbuttoned to show a claret-coloured silk waistcoat with a gold watch chain hanging from the fob pocket. 'I gave birth to the infant, as Mr Trelawny of Macquarie Street will testify if you care to ask him.'

'I am an American physician, ma'am.'

Sarah Dyer rolls her eyes, as if to say she has never heard of such an unlikely combination and is inclined to doubt the truth of it. 'Then you must meet 'im, sir, Mr Trelawny that is, and admire his leeches.' She flattens out the creases in her skirt and adds coquettishly, 'You are too late to explore for yourself, and will have to take Trelawny's word for it.'

Banes takes another turn around the room, pausing to poke the fire with his stick. 'Never mind Trelawny, ma'am. I dare say there's literature on the subject. Documents and sightings and affidavits duly witnessed by persons of quality. The law properly satisfied that the creature is what it purports to be.' He glances at Ned, then at his mother. 'I presume the law is satisfied, ma'am?'

'If you mean by that, sir, is the child a fraud, the magistrates could find no evidence of it, and would find none if they flogged it out of us, and if you don't believe me, sir, you may get out this minute.'

'Pardon, ma'am, I did not mean to give offence.' He stoops down to ruffle Ned's hair, causing the boy to flinch. 'Why, ma'am, the Lord has managed to put some singular things in a lady's womb and it ain't our business to question why.'

Mrs Dyer benevolently allows herself to forgive the offence.

'You was not violated, I hope,' he remarks delicately, 'in the course of this miracle.'

'No, sir, I wasn't. Now if you don't mind…'

But Banes does mind. He minds very much. He has gone to considerable trouble to come this far. He has soiled his coat, muddied his boots and endured an hour of tedious conversation from Mr Boxer. His curiosity has been tickled and his entrepreneurial spirits aroused. These are cultivated sentiments, much admired in his native Boston, and Banes has no intention of leaving before they are satisfied. He clears his throat. 'Is it true, ma'am, what it says on the notice, that the varmint can hold a tune?'

'He's none of your American varmints, mister, and I won't have him called one.'

'Begging your pardon again, ma'am.' Banes fingers his waistcoat pocket for a coin. 'Only I'd be much obliged to hear the young crittur.' He pinches a silver half dollar between his thumb and forefinger. 'I've been to London twice and I never in that fine city laid eyes on a pup that sang.'

'We don't need your London tales, sir, to be proud of Arthur.'

'Arthur, ma'am? Is that the individual's name? I declare it has a ring to it. I'd surely like to hear Arthur.' He places the silver coin on the table. 'If it ain't too much trouble.'

Mrs Dyer, after a suitable delay, pockets the coin. 'He might manage a verse, if you insist.'

'A verse, ma'am, is all I ask.'

And a verse is all he gets, a short one at that, just a few bars of a sailor's hornpipe, but it's enough for Dr Benjamin Banes to smell money.

~

THE ROAD to York Plains, which is the road to Bagdad and Muddy Plains and Jericho, and everywhere in between, follows the right bank of the River Derwent past Mount Direction as far as the ragged hamlet of Herdsman's Cove, where it forks right along the Jordan River towards Broad Marsh and the farms around Green Ponds.

The road peters to a muddy path, scarcely more than a goat track, skirting marshes and running through water-logged pastures before striking out across a grass plain towards Spring Hill and Jericho.

Seeing the hands of his silver watch inching towards ten o'clock, the Reverend Mr Kidney takes a couple of biscuits from his satchel and swigs down a mouthful of brandy. The potentially ominous implications of the latter act are not lost on the horse, which throws up its head at the whiff of brandy and swipes the chaplain against some overhanging foliage.

The high grey clouds which delivered a few drops of rain have now dispersed, leaving an expanse of blue sky ahead. It occurs to the chaplain that this errand, with its attendant thoughts and observations, will furnish him with the material for a weighty sermon on the subject of Christian charity. Moistening his lips with another swig, he attempts the beginnings of such a sermon on an audience of trees and tussock grass.

There are sheep and horned cattle grazing near the road. From time to time, the chaplain sees kangaroos spring out of the low scrub spilling down the wooded hills to his left. They stop and stare before hopping away, brushing the scrub with the backs of their paws.

The kangaroos remind the chaplain of an engraving, shown to him by Mr Sculley, of a sooterkin, done by a Dutch artist in the town of Nijmegen after a description by the local pastor.

The kangaroo seems to him, if anything, the odder of the two creatures. Its shape is more peculiar, its motion more unorthodox. It bears little resemblance, in either appearance or habits, to any other of God's creatures. But while taxidermy can verify the existence of the kangaroo nobody, to Mr Kidney's knowledge, has yet succeeded in stuffing a sooterkin.

Looking up at the horizon, the chaplain notices pools of sunlight glowing strangely on a snow-capped mountain. The island has always seemed surreal in its extremes of climate and geography, its odd effects of light and shadow, its macabre coalescence of the familiar and the unknown. Here is a meadow, hardly different from a meadow in Oxfordshire or Bedfordshire, but for the kangaroo. There a stream such as you might find in any English village, except for the platypus swimming in its shallows.

The road carries him over rushing brown cataracts bridged with logs, or forded with moss-covered stepping stones. Sometimes he sees fat mottled trout swimming just below the surface or leaping to snap up a fly. They alert him to the approach of midday and hence the desirability of lunch. A trout (grilled, with butter and burnt almonds) would suit him nicely. Or, failing that, a casserole of mutton.

He looks about in search of a farmhouse. The nearest dwelling is a convict stockman's hut, distinguishable by a smudge of brown smoke from a damp fire. Even this would require a cross-country detour of several miles. Such a diversion would be rewarded, at best, with a plate of stale bread and cheese. Mr Kidney unbuckles his satchel and settles instead for a chunk of salt pork. His plump fingers feel instinctively for the brandy flask. He registers the unexpected lightness of the flask before removing the stopper. The warm brandy slides down his throat and ripples through the furred arteries that blossom into a spiderweb of burst capillaries in his nose.

Gazing ahead at the forest spreading like a thick carpet over the hills, the chaplain turns his thoughts towards the timber trade. He has raised the subject several times in his letters to Lord Spencer, alluding vaguely to risks and costs, and vigorously to volumes and receipts, and proposing a modest investment by his lordship of, say, five hundred guineas, with the profits to be shared equitably between them. Equitably, in the chaplain's mind, amounting to a round figure (say, one hundred pounds per annum) which would enable him to wipe out his most compromising debts, and save him (he hopes) from the necessity of contracting more.

The figures, as they have been explained to him, seem irresistibly attractive. She-oak timber will fetch twenty shillings a ton in Hobart Town. There are X tons of wood per acre and Y million acres. Calculating the total volume of timber by the market price, Mr Kidney has obtained a figure equal to the entire national debt of Great Britain, needing nothing more than a steady influx of free settlers to achieve it. The equation seems childishly simple, the resource inexhaustible, the risks infinitesimal, the profits boundless—yet Lord Spencer has never replied to his proposal. Perhaps, thinks Mr Kidney, if one of these soaring eucalypts could be sent to him...

Occasionally the road veers sharply or divides in a fork before becoming one path again a mile or two ahead. Sometimes it dissolves into a muddy track. Now and then it vanishes altogether, forcing him to retrace his steps in order to find it again.

There are no signs to warn the unwary traveller. Flooding sometimes makes one route impassable, some-times another. Since the government surveyor rarely takes the trouble to maintain his work, there is no absolute author-ity to pronounce which path is the true one, and which the imposter, so the road has evolved by itself, heading off in new directions according to the damage it sustains each winter.

In severe winters, each detour spawns fresh detours, which then spawn detours of their own, like the muddy tributaries in a river delta, so that a man looking ahead at the endless scrub and straggly forest, even if he has made the trip countless times before, might find it impossible to know whether he is on the main road or not.

This year rain and melting snow have submerged large tracts of the road, while other parts have miraculously escaped damage. The section Mr Kidney is travelling is wide and muddy and carries a recent impression of cart-wheels. The driver of the cart was either drunk or in a great hurry. There are broken bottles, spindles of coloured cotton and odd items of kitchenware strewn along the way.

Once or twice the chaplain is tempted to stop and pick up a saucepan to give to Mrs Jakes on his return. Were he to dismount he could hardly fail to notice other tracks. He might even see the odd powder cartridge lying in the mud and come to the conclusion that the driver was being pursued by bushrangers.

There are wooded hills on his right; on his left, the swollen Jordan River, and beyond that, to the north-west, a range of jagged mountain peaks. From Mr Duffy's stockyards at Green Ponds the chaplain expects to see the lopsided hump of Spring Hill straight ahead of him, with the meandering course of the Coal River curling away to his right. His progress has been slower than he intended. Nevertheless, he will be more than halfway to York Plains and (he pulls out his silver watch) capable of reaching the farm comfortably before dusk.

Wooded hills on the right; mountains on the left. Mr Kidney steadies himself with another swig of brandy, and nudges his horse to the right, skirting a bog in which the rotting carcass of a sheep is visible, and then, several miles further on, to the right again, avoiding the floodplain of a winding creek. In the course of these manoeuvres he fails to notice that the road has shrunk to a track, and that the track is turning back on itself, until the wooded hills are directly in front of him and finally on his left.

The chaplain presses on, sneaking the occasional mouthful of brandy to ward off the afternoon chill, raising himself a few inches out of the saddle and farting with the sombre resolve of a man alone with his bowels.

A quarter of an hour slides by, and another. Mr Kidney becomes aware that the hills and mountains have switched sides, and everything is opposite to what it should be. Some things look too near and others too far away. The mountains themselves seem to have moved.

He keeps going, blaming the aberrations of perspective and hoping that the landscape will somehow right itself. But the view only becomes more distorted. The track which had once been so clear now looks shifty and ill-defined, as though it had deliberately set out to mislead him. Finally it forks around a fallen tree and disappears, leaving him to gaze forlornly into the scrub.

He turns his horse around and begins to retrace his steps. The sky is darkening. He stares at the gums shedding their bark like giant lizards. For a moment he is overcome by a sense of terrible isolation. The country seems primordial, uncouth, devoid of any human presence save his own. There is no sound. No smoke. No wheel ruts or chopped timber or torn powder cartridges.

A pair of grey-green parrots bursts out of a tree, screeching as they swoop over his head. There is only a faint glow left in the sky. The chaplain calls out but immediately regrets it, fearing the motives of whoever might come to investigate. Nobody comes. He shouts again, more calmly this time, trying to sound like a man temporarily separated from companions who will soon come looking for him.

He swallows a mouthful of brandy, enough to loosen the fingers around his chest and conjure disembodied noises out of the darkness—the rustle of bushes, the squeak of a saddle, the swish of a tail.

As the chaplain fumbles for his weapon, a little girl rides

out of the trees, perched on the back of a grey mare. The horse is no more than a dull smudge moving under her. 'It's Pa,' she says proudly. ''E's dead.'

~

'WELL NOW,' says Sarah Dyer, wiping a greasy thumb on her apron. 'Look what the cat's brought in.' She turns to Ned. ''Tis a day for unwanted visitors, eh, boy?'

The gate squeaks on its hinges and William Dyer staggers up the path, bloated and beer-sodden, with his arm around a stranger. Someone has given Dyer a spotted neckerchief, which is tied off like a tourniquet.

It is just after dark and a chandler's warehouse is burning in Collins Street, casting a lurid orange glow across the evening sky. A pall of black smoke is rolling off the flames. The air is thick with the stink of ship's tar and burnt canvas. Ned's face is streaked with soot from having stood in the crowd watching the blaze. He gets up from the battered leather armchair in time to see his father clamber up the wooden step to the front door.

The stranger has thin rascally lips and pale blue, red-rimmed eyes that remind Ned of a jellyfish. He is wearing a tatty brown frockcoat and three-cornered hat and black trousers turned up past the ankles. The coat is buttoned to the neck, and there is a gash in it, and a dark stain that someone has tried to scrub out, and a host of other injuries that don't escape Sarah Dyer's attention as she eyes him through the window. She looks back to see that the pup is in its cot before letting Ned open the door.

The thin-lipped stranger moves aside to allow his host

to fall over the threshold. As Dyer struggles to his feet, the stranger steps over him, bowing to Sarah with a feigned courtesy that she waves away with a flick of her hand.

It is not the first time William Dyer has dragged a stranger home with him. If it's not the Bird-in-Hand, it's the Calcutta or the Bricklayer's Arms or the Cat and Fiddle or the Plough, feet up by the fire, sucking on his clay pipe, telling everyone how he lent a hand to the midwife, and which end came first, and how the infant looks just like its mother, except for the whiskers, and slipped out like a trout, and whatever else comes into his head over a pint of mulled ale and a tumbler of rum. Then it's home, trudging up the hill arm in arm with a man he's never met before, falling over the step and demanding to know what's for supper.

Sarah Dyer looks at the stranger as if he were some curious specimen hauled up in a net. 'Is he eating?' she asks.

'He'll have roast beef, won't you, er, er...'

'He'll have chops, like the rest of us.'

'Chops'll do nicely, missus,' replies the thin-lipped man, without being asked. Squinting at the cot in the corner, he takes a step towards it, then turns around, smiling.

'You'll take that hat off,' Sarah says sharply.

'I'll keep it on, missus—if you don't mind.'

Sarah looks from the stranger to her husband and back again. 'Suit yourself.'

'Chops'll do nicely,' says Dyer, grinning stupidly while he wrestles with the rag around his neck. He pulls so hard at the knot that his eyes fill with tears and Sarah has to ungag him.

Dyer sits at one end of the table and his new chum at

the other. The stranger looks at Ned and asks, 'Were you at the fire, boy?'

'Where else would he have blackened himself,' snaps Sarah.

The man's pale blue eyes narrow and the lids come down until they're nothing but slits. 'Whose place was it?'

'Chaney's,' says Ned.

The stranger nods to himself and starts shovelling pork and pumpkin into his mouth like someone who hasn't seen food for a week, saving the fat until last and smacking his thin lips until they're glistening with grease. Every so often he looks around the room, as though admiring the stylishness of the accommodation, but always his gaze comes back to the cot with its snoring bundle of blankets. When he's finished he licks the knife and scrapes the gristle into a heap and gnaws the last strings of meat off the bones and says, 'That was a fine generous supper, missus.'

'You're welcome to it, I'm sure.'

The stranger lets out a satisfied belch as Sarah Dyer pushes a scalding mug of tea under his nose.

William Dyer looks up from his plate and says, through a mouthful of pumpkin, 'You'll stay for a pipe.'

'I would,' replies the stranger, 'only tobacco gives me the gripe.'

Dyer's eyes open wide, as if he's just seen a dog with two heads. He lays down his knife and fork and pushes the plate away with half a chop still uneaten. A trickle of gravy dribbles down his chin and gets lost in his beard. He wipes his mouth on his sleeve. 'I never heard of a man that smoked himself into the gripe,' he says.

The stranger shrugs and slurps his tea. His gaze drifts

back to the cot. He notices but fails to remark on a black flipper protruding from the blankets. 'I met a fellow once,' says Dyer, 'that was slapped so hard he swallowed his pipe. I heard he passed it whole a day later and was none the worse for it.'

The stranger smiles another oily smile at Sarah Dyer. 'Well, mister,' she says, 'may we know your business?'

He looks at her, then at Ned, and answers, 'Whales.'

'Oh?' says Sarah, expressing surprise. 'I heard the whales was all exhausted and those that ain't dead have swum away.'

'That is the common wisdom, missus.' He glances at Dyer, who leans back and scratches his belly like a walrus. 'But there is still some in the bays, if a man knows where to look.'

'Is that so?'

The stranger declines to add to his answer except by slurping his tea.

'Then,' says Sarah, 'you must know more than the others that packed up and left a month ago.'

The stranger smiles as if acknowledging a compliment. 'Much obliged to you, missus, for the handsome meal.' He gets up from the table and attempts to clamp an avuncular hand on Ned's shoulder, which Ned shakes off. 'There are gentlemen expecting me that cannot be kept waiting.' He casts a last furtive glance at the seal pup and, without waiting for the door to be opened, opens it himself and slips out into the darkness.

'He's up to no good,' says Mrs Dyer, but her husband is already asleep.

~

Whereas ROBERT LEFEBURE alias QUINCY, a Frenchman, one of the Crew of the Ship Ann, deserted from his Duty some Weeks ago, and is yet absent:—Any Person who shall apprehend the said Deserter and lodge him in Prison, will receive a Reward of Four Pounds Sterling from Mr BIRCH in Macquarie-street. The said Frenchman is about 5 feet 6 inches high, of a pink Complexion, and scarred beneath the left Ear.

~

DR BENJAMIN Banes has one of those faces that changes colour at the thought of money. The blood rushes to his head and suffuses his cheeks with a coppery glow. His moustache looks sharper and brighter. His eyes widen and the fine vertical lines on either side of his mouth deepen into slots the exact width of an American dollar. His pulse beats faster, his voice rises a semitone and everything about him suggests a man with a glittering fortune ahead of him, and a private appointment to meet it.

Banes is standing before the oval mirror in his cabin gripping an ivory-handled shaving razor which will shortly enjoy the privilege of trimming the bristles under his nose. The doctor views every one of his toilet items as being singularly honoured: the badger brush, the engraved silver soap holder, the crystal jar and atomiser filled with French lavender water, and the tiny pair of nail scissors given to him by a Russian nobleman who died of typhoid fever while visiting Boston. He picks them up and puts them down with a brisk formality that implies they are lucky to be touched at all.

The ship is moving with the swell and Banes moves expertly with it. He swipes at the luxuriant white lather on his upper lip, revealing a self-satisfied smile which has been playing around the edges of his mouth since dawn. Banes has spent the previous evening and all night locked in his cabin. There is dandruff on his shoulders which, on any normal day, would have been brushed off. But this morning Banes has no time for brushing.

Next to the lamp in his cabin is a leatherbound notebook, open at a page of calculations scribbled in red and black ink. On the facing page is a list of American cities. Some are written in capitals (NEW YORK, BOSTON, PHILADELPHIA, RICHMOND, NORFOLK) and the rest in plain script (Hartford, New Haven, Alexandria, Bethlehem). There's a figure in American dollars beside each city, with a question mark against it. Most of the numbers have been revised and rewritten several times.

Unusually for such a fastidious man, there are breadcrumbs and spots of gravy on the pages, suggesting that Banes has offended against the careful order which is the hallmark of his existence. Banes has eaten two, if not three meals without disturbing his calculations. At the bottom of the right-hand page, circled in black ink, are two figures signifying the upper and lower limits of what he stands to make from the commercial venture encrypted in his columns.

Banes chisels away at the bristles in the cleft of his upper lip, then flicks the lather off with his forefinger and watches it dissolve in the basin of water. The smile widens into a grin broad enough to reveal a glint of gold among his yellowing teeth.

Having removed every unwanted whisker, Banes submerges his face in the basin and dabs his cheeks with a towel and splashes himself with lavender water.

Adding a mustard-coloured cravat to his shirt, he buttons himself into his second-best frockcoat (the lining has been eaten out by moths and there is a patch stitched on the underside of the collar), adds a pair of gloves and a scarf against the wind, and pauses to admire the finished article in the mirror.

To say that Banes is pleased with himself will not do justice to the feelings which are racing through his finely tuned nervous system. Banes is always pleased with himself. He's pleased with himself for the simple fact that he is not somebody else. If men were obliged to bid for the privilege of being Dr Benjamin Banes, Banes would immediately put his hand up for ten thousand dollars and consider it a bargain.

The immediate cause of his satisfaction is a cunning scheme guaranteed to make him a fortune; a scheme that grows better the more he thinks about it, and which could be put to work at once if certain other parties would agree to his terms.

Banes's idea is this: that the seal pup, properly vouched for by some Harvard medical men of his acquaintance, and insured with a reputable New York broker at ninety per cent of its book value, less depreciation, could prove a powerful draw in the public theatres of the United States of America.

He has gone over the figures a dozen times, weighed up the risks and returns, the cost of buying fish and hiring theatres, the danger of flood and fire and civil commotion. And his conclusion is that the plan is good for at least six thousand dollars a year after expenses, of which he will happily part with ten per cent (and unhappily with twelve) for the loan of the pup, to be deducted from receipts and sent to the parents, twice a year, in a strongbox.

Nothing remains but to visit them and obtain their consent. With this in mind he fills his purse with coins and, finding the captain's dining room unlocked, takes a half-full bottle of madeira, which he tops up with rum and water so as not to appear parsimonious.

Two sailors are hanging upside down from the figure-head, scrubbing away seagull droppings with long brooms. Another man is fishing over the side. Boxer, the bosun's mate, is puffing on a short pipe. Seeing Banes emerge on deck, Boxer stands up quickly and knocks his pipe out on his heel. It is clear the two men have an arrangement between them, and that Banes doesn't wish to draw attention to it. So Boxer sits down again, re-lights his pipe and blows a few absent puffs while Banes strolls around the rigging exhibiting a previously unsuspected fascination for knots and pulleys. Finally Banes takes off his hat, which Boxer takes to be a signal to extinguish his pipe and lower himself surreptitiously over the side to a waiting rowboat.

A minute later, Banes's left boot appears over the railing, followed by the rest of him, clambering down the rope ladder with a feline delicacy marred, at the end, by the sight of the bosun's mate tugging on his trouser cuffs to save him from falling into the harbour.

Once ashore, Banes dismisses him with a dime. It is less than twenty-four hours since he laid eyes on the pup and this time he has no use for Boxer. He stops to watch the trading brigs disgorging their loads onto wharves crowded

with convicts and soldiers and scavenging dogs. The stink
of smoke and rotting fish hangs over the settlement, a thick
gamey stew fermenting slowly in the sun. Banes nods as a
man in a black cape rattles past in a cart; raises his hat to
a red-faced boy selling parsnips; gives a pinch of tobacco
to an old woman with a crutch. A ribald remark draws snig-
gers from two private soldiers lounging against the doors
of the powder magazine. A wolfhound—the property of
the harbourmaster—sniffs at the legs of Banes's trousers.

He pauses to light his pipe. A column of marines
splashes past, led by a corporal who looks twice as vicious
as any convict Banes has ever seen: pug-nosed, gap-toothed,
with half his left ear bitten off.

At last, after several wrong turnings and brusque inquiries,
Banes finds the house, which has just acquired a new coat
of black paint over its rotten timbers. But the mountain of
chop bones is still there, and the gutters are still sagging, and
the crooked chimney looks as though a strong gust of wind
would send it crashing to the ground. The front door is open
and Sarah Dyer is sitting outside on a chair.

'Good morning, ma'am,' says Banes, removing his hat.
'I have a proposition that concerns the crittur.'

The sound of an American voice brings William out of
the house. Banes looks annoyed to see him. 'A pleasure to
meet you, sir,' he says, reaching inside his coat for the bottle
of madeira and handing it over. As Dyer removes the stopper, his Adam's apple starts moving in anticipation, sliding
up and down like the bubble in a spirit level.

'We did not expect you back so soon,' says Sarah.

Banes stares thoughtfully into his hat. 'In my experience, ma'am, a proposition is best acted on while it is warm.'

'And what,' asks Sarah, 'might be the bones of this proposition?'

'The bones of it is this: I have a great desire to show your infant to the world, by which I mean the United States of America, and most especially the merchant cities of that nation, which are holding their breath for such wonders as you, ma'am, have had the good fortune to suckle at your breast. In short, ma'am, I wish to take the crittur off your hands for a year, to astound the world and lay before a paying audience, for which privilege I am disposed to offer you the sum of three hundred American dollars.'

'Go away,' says Ned, standing in the doorway with the pup in his arms.

Banes smiles and fingers his pocket for a coin. 'A fine boy, ma'am. I never saw better.'

'Will he be harmed?' asks William Dyer. 'Only the missus will not have him harmed.'

'Harmed, sir? Why, the crittur...'

'Arthur,' says Sarah.

Banes acknowledges his mistake with a perfunctory bow. 'Why, ma'am, Arthur will be coddled and pampered and petted like a prince. I shall not permit a single whisker to be damaged.'

Ned crouches down beside his mother and whispers, 'Send him away, Mam.'

'Be quiet, boy,' snaps Dyer, attempting to pull him back.

'Of course, ma'am,' continues Banes, 'the agreement is subject to certain clauses and provisos, indemnities and whatnot...'

'Never mind them,' says Dyer.

'Well, ma'am?' asks Banes. 'Is the sum sufficient?

I believe there may be room for negotiation.'

'No.'

'Four hundred?'

'Arthur will stay where he is, Mr Banes. Ned could not bear to be parted from him.'

Banes endeavours to insert a silkily trousered leg between Ned and his mother. 'Perhaps you misheard, ma'am. I believe the sum mentioned was five hundred American dollars.'

'Done!' shouts William Dyer.

His wife frowns and says, 'We are happy as we are, Mr Banes. We want none of your American dollars, nor none of your politeness neither. Arthur is ours and no-one else'll touch him.'

Benjamin Banes shakes his head and, with a smile that suggests the game is not over, turns towards the gate.

~

ROBERT LEFEBURE alias Quincy finishes scraping his corns and slides the bone-handled knife into his trouser pocket. His thin lips are pinched even tighter than usual. He has a dark, angry-looking bruise under his left eye. There are flecks of blood on his collar and a sliver is missing from the lobe of his right ear. He has visited a barber, or been involved in a brawl, or both. Beside him, on the soiled blanket of a rusty iron bed, is a crumpled piece of paper which might turn out to be a copy of the reward poster, torn from the wall of the Customs House.

The room is a bare, splintery place, more like a kennel, with thin walls reaching to within a foot of the ceiling and some latticework to fill the gap. There is a cracked porcelain jug in the corner, and a washstand (but no bowl), a tiny window nailed shut and a wooden chest that substitutes for a chair. There is no handle on the door, but unwanted visitors are kept out with a heavy padlock bolted to an iron bracket protruding from the door jamb. In the far corner of the room sits a polished wooden box, loosely packed with straw, with several holes drilled through the lid.

Quincy has hung his tatty brown coat on the back of the door. He does not appear perturbed by the announcement of a four-pound reward for his capture. He has, however, placed his shoes together on the trunk, facing the door, as if in readiness for a swift exit.

The fact is, there are too many men in the colony who need hunting and not enough men to hunt them. There are posters all over the island with names and ages and descriptions of missing persons. Prisoners absconded, soldiers deserted, wives and servants disappeared. Convicts who vanish just to give themselves up and split the reward with the finder. Drowned men and murdered men whose bodies will never be found. It can be assumed that Quincy jumped ship in the belief that nobody would bother looking for him.

Human noises float over the walls, fretful snores, feverish moans, the grunt of a man battering away at a whore for sixpence. The sounds and smells of a dingy boarding house at the harbour end of Argyle Street. No-one is eager here to know anyone else's business, or reveal their own.

It's Tuesday evening and the small, dusty window is streaked with drizzle. The melted stump of a candle is burning in a jar, throwing just enough light on the uneven wooden floor to reveal a trail of bloodspots, still wet, leading from the bed to the washstand, ending in what looks like a pile of rags, so filthy as to blend invisibly into the floorboards.

If you hold a candle over the porcelain jug, you'll see that the water is red, and there are clumps of black hair floating in it which, until an hour ago, were sprouting from Quincy's head. And tufts of grey-brown fur belonging to the rabbit whose bones are wrapped in the bundle of rags on the floor. Nearby is a sailmaker's needle with a length of catgut still threaded to it. All of which suggests that Quincy, besides cutting his hair and scraping his corns and sewing a large pouch into his overcoat, has spent the afternoon gutting a rabbit, stuffing it with sawdust and shot, and stitching it up again, for reasons best known to himself.

Meanwhile the finest part of the rabbit, a juicy fillet, is stewing in a pot in the kitchen, watched by the landlady and her invalid husband, who whistles obligingly whenever an unfamiliar face walks past.

~

AT A few minutes after nine o'clock, with oil lamps blazing in hotel windows and ships' lanterns swinging and braziers hissing in the rain, Ned stumbles in with the pup's trouser leg hanging limp over his shoulder.

'What's become of your father?' asks Sarah Dyer. 'He will drink himself to death.' Suddenly she catches sight of the pup's empty trouser leg. 'God save us, boy. What have you done with Arthur?'

Ned stares at her, trembling, mouth agape, like a fish suffocating on a rock.

Sarah grabs him by the shoulders. 'Speak to me, child. Where is Arthur? What have you done with him? Has your father got him?'

Ned is so overwhelmed with grief that he can barely get the words out. 'It w-w-weren't my f-fault, Mam.'

'Never mind whose fault. Where is he?'

'I never t-took me eyes off him, only for h-half a second...'

There is something clenched in his fist: a freshly stuffed rabbit skin, sewn up and weighted with shot. Sarah snatches it savagely out of his hand. 'What's this, Ned?' She drops the rabbit skin and claps her hands to her cheeks, as if her face would fall away without them. 'Oh God, Ned, what's happened to him?'

'Someone t-took him, Mam. I never...'

But Sarah Dyer is already halfway to the gate. Ned staggers blindly after her. 'It weren't my fault, Mam...Mam... MAM!'

~

Sydney
New South Wales

Sir,

I write in immediate response to your letter which, I must conclude, was subject to malicious interference after it left your hands, in consequence of which the wax was broken and the contents corrupted. I see no other explanation for the Tittle-tattle (I refuse to dignify it with any

other word) that comprises the greater part of the corre-
spondence. I refer to the abortion which, by the tendency
and explicit purpose of your letter, you have seen fit to
attribute to the infinite Mercy of God, instead of to the
enterprise (hardly less infinite) of Human Mischief upon
Human Gullibility.

You should scarcely need telling that you inhabit a
colony of convicts, for whom Truth and Honesty are
open liabilities, and Duplicity a passport to Profit, and
furthermore that there is no creature so devious as a
woman with child, whether the child be conceived in
Shame or Honour.

I have been informed that your own housekeeper was
engaged for the delivery, and must therefore be either Party
or Witness to the stratagem by which the Deformity was
brought into the world. I urge you to subject this female
without delay to the severest interrogation in order to
unmask the Perpetrator of the Fraud. Any weakness in this
matter would constitute a grave dereliction, for which you
must bear the consequences.

It behoves me to remind you that your tenure as
Chaplain is a fragile one; that you have more implacable
Foes than indomitable Friends, and that the greater mass
of the Colony would no more lament your going than
they would (as I hear) forgive your Debts. If I must speak
plain, Kidney, you are not indispensable, and had better
remember it.

As to the parcel that accompanied your letter, whatever
specimen it contained was incompetently preserved for such
a journey and the greater part of the Creature was
destroyed by vermin. That which remained was merely Fur

and Bones, which proved of passing interest to my dog, but none whatever to me.

I am, Sir, your obdt servant, etc.

Revd Saml Marsden

~

SHORTLY BEFORE midnight, William Dyer creeps home from the Bird-in-Hand with a hangdog look on his face. He hardly notices Ned slumped among the weeds outside the gate, but paces around the yard for an hour in the dark before slouching indoors, leaving Sarah to search for the pup alone.

Ned expects a whipping. He expects to be taken by the collar and bent over a stump and thrashed unmercifully with a leather slipper. A beating like that will satisfy his father but it won't make Ned feel any better. And it won't bring the pup back.

He sits by the gate all night, waiting for it to happen. But his father merely looks at him in a baleful sort of way and shakes his head, as though whatever punishment is coming will be inflicted with something more terrible than a leather slipper.

By the time she comes home, just before dawn, Sarah is convinced she will never see her pup again. The talk around the wharves is that Arthur is on his way to Brazil to be sold in the markets, or that he's been skinned by sealers or left for dead in the woods. Her face is fixed in a look of despair, as pale as one of Mr Sculley's plaster casts.

~

DURING TUESDAY night a thick fog rolls down the slopes of Mount Wellington, enveloping trees and blanketing gardens and pooling in the shallow bays of the harbour. As dawn comes up a handful of rowboats can be seen wallowing in the gloom, oared by gaunt figures who might be shrimpers or lobstermen.

The brig *Henrietta*, having ridden in on the last high tide, is tied up at the wharf. The handful of convicts not actively going about their work are actively shirking it, shuffling their feet and nodding and peering into the fog as if anticipating the arrival of some immense schooner.

One figure appears disengaged from the business of loading and unloading, stacking and shifting, rolling and carrying. A thin-lipped man in a tatty brown frockcoat is loitering near the gangplank, trying to interest the crew in a property which has lately come into his possession—a bundle that would fetch one hundred guineas on the streets of London or Amsterdam, but which he is prepared to sell for twenty.

The harbourmen don't trust him. A couple ask to see the parcel with their own eyes. The thin-lipped man says he has got it hidden away to keep it safe from thieves. A couple of guineas is the most he's offered. He worms up to a party of sealers unloading skins from a jolly-boat. They're not interested but they know a man who might be. A trader, camped somewhere up the coast, near Oyster Bay.

The stranger would rather get rid of the property at once. He drops his price. There are no takers. He sets off to try his luck among the hunchbacked boarding houses behind the wharves.

An hour later the Derwent ferryman is roused by the

noise of a pistol butt hammering on his door. The traveller asks to be taken across the river. He is leading a black mare and has a bulge under his coat.

The ferryman looks him over, taking careful note of the pistol stuffed in his belt. He remarks that timbercutters are working in the valley and that sawlogs have been sliding by all week. He says that these sawlogs make it hazardous to attempt a crossing in the fog. He speculates that the fog might not lift for an hour or more, and suggests making use of one of the log bridges upriver.

Since, however, the gentleman is plainly in a hurry, the ferryman tucks some tobacco into his pipe and inquires what such a hurry might be worth.

~

THE REVEREND Mr Kidney, having come too late to usher William Wheeler into heaven, is determined to see his daughter provided for. He buries the farmer amid a stoic and tuneless gathering of neighbours, several of whom are indecently anxious to know the terms of his will.

All week he rides from farm to farm, wheedling, cajoling, insisting that some refuge be found for the girl. The same neighbours who mourned the father's death now seem indifferent to the fate of the child. It enters Mr Kidney's head that if some taker cannot be found he will have no choice but to carry her back with him and deposit her among the government orphans who, on account of their looks or temperament, have forfeited the sympathies of Hobart society. The thought of condemning the girl to such a future is a distasteful one.

On Saturday he rides out again, fortified by half a pint of brandy and the greater part of a leg of mutton. He goads, threatens, demands that someone take her in, and in the end someone does, an elderly widow, enlisted with a promise (unlikely to be honoured) of money and clothes from the orphaned children's fund. His duty done, and the last of the brandy gone, the Reverend Mr Kidney sleeps soundly. The next morning he helps himself to a bottle of Wheeler's rum and, after an unhurried breakfast, turns his horse for Hobart Town, pleased to have saved himself the trouble of a Sunday sermon.

The road is no more than three miles away, behind some craggy hills. He wonders whether, in light of his earlier disorientation, it would be sensible to obtain precise directions from a neighbour. No doubt it would. But the nearest neighbour being several miles away, the weather congenial, and the rum rather better than he supposed, he decides he can do without them. Wheeler's daughter contrived to avoid a swollen creek by riding around it. Mr Kidney's plan is to save himself unnecessary mileage by crossing it.

Since he doesn't ask, nobody thinks it necessary to tell him of the timber bridge that was washed away in the winter floods, or warn him of the risks of attempting to cross by the ford, which has grown faster and deeper as a result of heavy snowfall on the mountains, and would give pause to a better horseman than Mr Kidney.

In any case, Mr Kidney is in no mood to heed such warnings. Discovering the shattered remains of the bridge, he rides upstream in search of the ford, observing that others have recently done the same, and concluding that it must therefore be safe.

The ford proves to be deeper than he was expecting. The current is faster. The chaplain takes his horse to the edge of the water and dismounts.

The bank is crowded with willows. A frayed rope, which would have assisted him in crossing the ford, now dangles uselessly from a low branch. An identical rope hangs from a tree on the opposite bank.

Mr Kidney's piebald gelding affirms that it will not, under any circumstances, enter the water, and takes command of the situation by leading the chaplain to the edge of a clearing dominated by two massive lichen-covered boulders. A myrtle tree, encrusted with staghorns, stands at the end of the clearing. Sensing an imminent battle of wills, Mr Kidney addresses the beast by name, intimating that delightful rewards or, alternatively, heinous retribution will flow from its decision. Nelson drops his head and starts pulling at the wet grass.

It soon becomes apparent, even to the chaplain's unobservant eyes, that the clearing has been visited by others. He sees a pair of moccasin shoes hanging from a branch a few feet from where his horse is grazing, and a set of white skittles scattered about the grass, like the bleached bones of a cow. He looks around, half expecting whoever left them to stroll out of the shadows with an impromptu invitation for lunch.

But no invitation appears. Nor, he realises, is one likely to appear. So he circles the horse, rubbing his hands in a manner intended to convey his determination to press on without delay. The animal glances up at him, a string of green spittle swinging from its chin. Its expression seems to imply a readiness to continue the journey, provided that

Mr Kidney can find a stump from which to remount.

Heaving himself into the saddle, he pauses to inspect the moccasins and is suddenly conscious of voices sniggering. He gropes for the fowling piece on his shoulder. 'Hello?' he calls out. 'Is anyone there?'

On the far side of the clearing, a bay mare strolls out of the undergrowth, unsaddled but with a bridle still over its head.

The chaplain's stomach, bulging with porridge and salt pork, turns over inside him. He hears raucous laughter in the bushes, the squeak of leather boots, the swipe of a sword coming out of its scabbard.

The bay mare advances slowly, rolling its head from side to side, paying no more than passing attention to the chaplain and his gelding.

More laughter. The crack of a branch. A drunken curse. A thunderous belch.

'Who's there?' The chaplain points his gun at the mare, at the trees, at the boulders, as if they are equally threatening.

'Very well, Mr Kidney,' says a voice behind him, 'you may put away your piece.'

The chaplain takes a moment to grasp the proposition, then drops the gun at once, without looking around.

'I said put it away, damn you, not drop it.'

'P-pardon me,' he stutters. He tries to turn round, but is stopped by a fierce prod from a musket.

'Lost, are we?' asks the voice.

Mr Kidney shifts in his saddle. 'Not lost, sir. Not lost at all…I, er, know very well where I am. I was merely watering my horse before proceeding on my journey to…' He stops himself. 'I have friends nearby.'

'Savages, are they?'

'I beg your pardon?'

'You won't find any Englishmen here to sing your hymns.' There are guffaws from two or three companions. Mr Kidney keeps looking straight ahead of him. He now sees a canvas shelter, half hidden among the trees, with the trampled remains of a camp fire. A pair of boots is impaled on sticks, as if the man wearing them has burrowed headfirst into the ashes. He says circumspectly, 'Jericho is nearby, is it not?'

'No, Mr Kidney, it is not. Jericho is twenty miles away. Is Jericho your destination?'

'You address me very freely. Do I know you, sir?'

'By reputation, I dare say. Perhaps you have read my name in the newspaper.'

The chaplain ponders the meaning of this remark, which seems to contain some veiled threat. 'If you would consent, sir, to show me the road to Jericho, I shall be happy to leave you in peace.'

'In peace, will you? I'm sure my friends here will be glad of it.'

'Then, sir, if you will allow me...'

'Get off the horse, Kidney.'

'I will stay, if you don't mind.'

'Dismount.'

The chaplain hesitates, then lowers himself clumsily to the ground, taking care not to let go of the reins. He hears a rustle of leaves to his right.

Another voice says, 'That's a decent-looking pair of breeches, Kidney. Would you take five guineas for them?'

'I have need of them myself, sir. I have no other clothes, or I would gladly part with them.' He turns his head slightly to the right. 'Come, gentlemen, I am already delayed in my business. If I can be of no service to you, then I must be on my way.'

'Service, Kidney?' says the first voice. 'And what service is that? Perhaps you consider us ripe for baptising?'

'Or burying,' quips another.

'Very good, Daniel. I believe Mr Kidney here would bury us tastefully.'

The chaplain, forgetting what he was told, turns round to see a red-haired, pug-nosed lieutenant. His scarlet tunic has one epaulette torn off, a button missing and gold braid hanging loose from the shoulders. He is holding not a musket but a candlestick. The other men, a private and a corporal, are similarly dishevelled. The lieutenant is wearing a sturdy pair of black boots; the others have kangaroo moccasins.

The lieutenant spits contemptuously on the ground. 'What are you doing here, Kidney?' he growls.

Had the officer's uniform been in a more respectable condition, the chaplain would have tried to shake his hand. Even now he is tempted to make the gesture, if only because of the wolfish looks of his companions. The vicious habits of the common soldier are enough to recommend the company of even the most debauched officer. But something stops him. He stares at the lieutenant, whose gilt gorget plate, he notices, is sitting back to front. Slowly it dawns on him that they might not be soldiers after all.

The red-haired man, Michael Brodie, grins back at him. 'This is dangerous country to be out in, Kidney. The savages are loose and God will not protect your churchman's arse from a spear.' He bends down to pick up Mr Kidney's fowling piece. 'You will be safe from parrots, at least.' After examining the firing mechanism, he tosses the chaplain his weapon. 'But you must discover how to load it first.'

Mr Kidney finds the loss of his honorific unaccountably shocking—more shocking than being poked in the back with a musket. Looking around, he glimpses a wooden chest lying broken on the grass and various garments draped over bushes. 'I repeat, sir, if you would be so generous as to point me towards my destination, I shall not trouble you further.'

'A gentleman of the cloth is no trouble, as long as he keeps his prayers to himself.' Brodie bends down to feel the gelding's legs. 'My feeling is, Kidney, that you will be safer remaining with us.'

'Safer?'

'The woods are full of bushrangers. We have had skirmishes already.' He pulls open his tunic to reveal a bloody bandage. 'Why, Kidney, my friend Mr Watts almost had his balls shot off.' Watts, holding his crotch, indicates that the shot missed.

The chaplain nods a little too eagerly and says, 'I appreciate your concern, sir, and was hoping to have prevailed on you for an escort'—he puts the fowling piece over his shoulder—'but I see your numbers are too few. I assure you, gentlemen, your courage will not go unreported'—he glances at the bay mare, wondering if there are other horses concealed among the trees—'I am certain Mr Bent will find room in his columns for your exploits. Unfortunately I am not as agile as I was...' He grips the saddle with both hands while his left boot gropes for the stirrup. The horse promptly begins to walk away. 'If one of you gentlemen will lend me a hand...'

Nobody moves.

Brodie lifts the gelding's head and runs his thumb along the animal's gums. 'It seems they will have you stay to supper.'

'Supper? It is but three hours since breakfast!'

'Then, Mr Kidney, we shall have to make a day of it.'

~

SARAH WON'T talk to Ned. She can't even look at him without crying. She takes to her bed and won't get up, and won't eat, and won't open her mouth except to wish she was dead. The blackest oaths are lost on her husband, who spends most of the day immersed in a cloud of tobacco smoke and most of the night with his face in a pot of ale. But Ned feels as though his heart has been pulled out whole.

Before long there are mobs in the street, foul-mouthed sailors and gaudy whores and layabout ticket-of-leave men, mocking them for the loss of the seal pup, and asking if they can't hatch another the same.

Ned finds a seal pelt on the step, and a trail of blood leading to the gate. Sarah cries out when she sees it, a terrible noise like the howl of a lost calf. But Ned knows it's not their pup. It doesn't have the eyes or the whiskers or the scar it got from sniffing William Dyer's clay pipe as it glowed on the step. It doesn't have the scabs on its nose from being pricked by sea urchins, or the bump on its head from Mr Sculley's callipers. It has none of the marks that are as familiar to Ned as the scabs on his own knees and the scrapes on his knuckles. So he picks the pelt up and throws it in the street, where the bullock carts trundle over it until it is torn and buried in the mud and even the dogs won't go near it.

Sarah Dyer sits like a ghost in her crumpled nightdress, with her hands in her lap and her white face staring out the window. William eyes her in a hurt, hungover sort of way and wanders off to get drunk.

~

WILLIAM WHEELER, a Farmer, of York Plains, died on Monday last of a Fever. The Illness had resisted all Cures, and its Virulence rendered the sorrowful Outcome inevitable. Mr WHEELER was renowned by all who knew him for his Virtuous Character and Generous Disposition. He was recently widowed and leaves a Daughter to bewail his Death. Mr KIDNEY's sober Presence must no doubt be an immeasurable Comfort to the bereaved Child.

~

AT THE top of Argyle Street is a pottery with a tall brick chimney and at the back of the pottery is a shed where sacks of charcoal are stored. The iron padlock is old and stiff and Ned can pick it with his eyes shut, a trick he learned from Mr Goldfarb. The shed has no windows but the light falling through the chinks in the walls is enough to see by.

Mr Isaac Goldfarb was transported for forgery, served three years and was let out on a ticket of leave. He is a small clever man with heavy eyebrows and a limp that can't decide which leg it belongs to, or whether it belongs to both at once. Mr Goldfarb is much affected by chilblains and never comes to the shed without taking off his shoes and rubbing goose fat between his toes. If it were not for chilblains, he says, he would be out cutting timber or shifting sacks of grain or hauling stone for the causeway. But a man racked with chilblains is a danger to himself and others, and that is why he can't labour and must live on his brains instead.

Mrs Goldfarb is dead and left behind in the Whitechapel fog. She would die again (says Goldfarb, picking wax out of his ear) to see him suffer, which is the fate of every poor London Jew with no wife to keep him, and no job, and no roof over his head.

Not that Mr Goldfarb sleeps now, or has ever slept, outdoors. He sleeps in a boarding house behind the government bond store. But what stands between him and the sky does not, in his opinion, merit the name of a roof. It is a horsehair and plaster ceiling, poorly built and crudely repaired, through which the elements come and go as they please. On sunny days the ceiling glows from the light streaming through it. On wet days it leaves milky puddles on the floor. He pays the rent by writing petitions and drawing up wills for illiterate settlers.

Mr Goldfarb comes to the shed to steal charcoal, which he does by unstitching the sacks and replacing the missing pieces with seashells. He considers this a cunning trick, as charcoal and seashells sound identical when they are rattling in a sack and it's hard to tell them apart when they are cinders.

'And what's to stop a man burning seashells?' Mr Goldfarb asks rhetorically. 'Only this: seashells don't burn hot enough, which is why charcoal costs five shillings a bag and seashells cost nothing but the labour of picking them up.'

Ned and Mr Goldfarb are sitting in the shed listening to the wind blowing over the chimney. Ned wishes that he would stop talking about seashells and tell him how to get Arthur back, as he promised. From time to time he stops stitching and looks up imploringly, but Goldfarb merely shakes his head and carries on rubbing goose fat between his toes.

Goldfarb's toes are short and white, with long yellow nails, and won't stop wriggling. The more he rubs them, the harder they wriggle. They remind Ned of the worms his father uses to fish for eels in the rivulet, except Mr Goldfarb's toes are plumper.

Finally he stops rubbing and says in a slow solemn voice, 'You must use what's in here.' He leans over and screws his thumb into Ned's temple until it hurts. 'Intyvishun, boy. You must use your intyvishun. The more intyvishun the better.'

Ned scratches out a mangled spelling in the charcoal dust. 'Is that the same as brains?'

Mr Goldfarb wipes the fat off his fingers and puts on one of his shoes. 'It's better than brains, Ned. Brains'll show a boy what's in front of his nose, but intyvishun will let him see what's beyond it. Brains is what a boy needs to do ledgers and pick padlocks and learn the law, but brains won't help him find what was stolen from him when his back was turned. Brains is no good to you, Ned, for sniffing out rascals and catching swindlers, and if you had a hatful of brains and no intyvishun you'd be as good as a bull with no bollocks.'

'How do you know I've got it?'

'I don't know it, Ned, but I've a hunch. The Jews is blessed with great intyvishun and can tell it in a boy by looking.' He puts on his other shoe. 'You remember, Ned, when I gave you that pocket watch, and you lost it, and I says a clever boy can lose a dozen pocket watches and still know what time it is.'

'Yes,' says Ned.

'Well what time is it?'

No answer.

'Go on, boy. Tell me the time.'

Ned squints through a crack in the wall. 'I reckon it's just gone five o'clock.'

'Why, Ned?'

'Because the man that comes to guard the clay pots has gone to fetch his kettle.'

Mr Goldfarb gets to his feet and pushes the sacks against the wall. 'Intyvishun ain't knowing the answer, boy. It's knowing where to look for it.' He pats the charcoal in his pockets, as if he can feel it warming up already. 'Intyvishun will get Arthur back. You see if it doesn't.' He opens the door a few inches and peers through the crack. 'Now wait here till I'm gone, and shut the door after you.' He squashes his thumb against Ned's temple and hisses, 'Intyvishun!'

By now the sky is darkening and the air is smutty with cinders. There is brown smoke wheezing from the ticket-men's huts in Argyle Street and braziers spitting out sparks and tallow torches stinking. If you shut your eyes you'd think the whole settlement was catching fire.

There is one hearth that isn't lit and that's Ned's. The

front door is open but there is nobody home, only a dog sniffing under the bed that scampers out when it sees him. Ned flops down in his father's armchair with a plate of bread and dripping he can hardly bring himself to eat, shuts his eyes and wishes he could hear the pup snoring in its cot.

But the cot is gone, thrown outside and left to warp in the rain. Ned feels the tears welling up in his eyes. He sniffs and wipes his nose with his knuckles. He waits for the intyvishun to speak, as Mr Goldfarb swore it would, but all it says is the dripping has gone rancid. As Ned tosses his crusts on the fire he notices the pup's skittle lying half-burnt in the ashes. He goes to bed knowing he must find Arthur or never come home again, and that he must do it by himself.

~

A Mystery envelops the Whereabouts of the Revd Mr KIDNEY, whose Admirers await his Return from York Plains. His Attendance had been expected at a Dinner for the Bible Society on Friday Night. No Intelligence has been forthcoming that might explain his Absence.

~

NED IS woken by a terrible moaning in the bed and finds his mother has crawled in beside him and wrapped herself around him like an octopus. She is dead to the world and doesn't stir as he wriggles out of her grasp. William Dyer is snoring in his armchair. There is a bottle of rum open on the table and oysters scattered about the floor and a lump of cheddar cheese wrapped in brown paper. Ned puts the cheese in his pocket and scribbles a brief note—'gon to find Arthur'—before shutting the door behind him.

It is dark outside. There is nobody awake but cocks and bakers' boys. The smell of hot bread reminds Ned that he has nothing to go with the cheese. So he steals half a loaf from an open window in Collins Street, together with some mussels and a ham bone and a knife left out for sharpening, and a pouch of shag tobacco and some other bits and pieces that might come in useful, and stuffs them all in a hessian sack.

As he crosses the bridge over the rivulet, a voice in his head whispers, 'Mr Swanton has a rowboat which is moored on the river a quarter mile from his house. You will have to paddle as the current is against you but keep to the middle where the water is deepest. A mile or two will do the trick then you can run it into the reeds and walk along the bank and no-one will ever know it was you that stole it.'

Until now it hasn't dawned on Ned to steal a boat. He has never rowed by himself and has no idea where the river will take him. He's not sure if it's brains or intyvishun but there's something inside telling him what to do and he knows he must follow.

The rowboat is waiting for him, tied to a stake with a length of muddy rope. The oars are hidden under a bush beside an empty gin bottle. There is dew on the grass and footprints leading into the woods which would end up sooner or later with Swanton's man, who has been smuggling grog on the river. At the sight of them Ned decides not to leave the boat in the reeds, as the voice told him, but to push it out so it will get beached on a sandbar downstream. That way there will be no footprints nearby and nobody will know if the thief went up or down or if the boat was stolen at all or just worked itself loose in the current.

Ned unties the rope and drops the oars in the boat. He puts one leg in and pushes off with the other, but the boat is stuck fast in the mud. Climbing out, he tries to turn it into the current, but still the river won't take it. So he crouches down and shoves the bow into the water. Suddenly the boat swings round and slips away without him, dragging the rope after it. Ned manages to grab the rope before it squirms out of reach, and the boat slews and runs aground on the bank. He scrambles back in. This time he pushes off with the oar and the rowboat glides into the river. He takes a last look at the bank, then chops his oars in the current, heaving on the left one, then on the right, then on both at once, until the boat is bucking gently through the water.

From time to time he catches a whiff of tobacco and hears men's voices murmuring in one of the ramshackle huts on the banks. Every once in a while a dog barks and Ned huddles down so he can't be seen.

Slowly he gets the rhythm of it and feels the current rippling under him. Before long the town is a mile behind. All he can see is the lights in the barracks and the glow of the torches outside the gaol and then darkness and then nothing, just the oars splashing and the black river winking in the moonlight.

But the current is stronger than it looks. Sometimes he seems not to be moving at all and sometimes the river drags him fishtailing back. Soon the sky is turning pink and Ned realises he has gone no more than a few hundred yards. He can see smoke curling from the pottery chimney and hear cattle lowing in the holding pens. So with a final effort he pulls himself over to the bank and jumps ashore, leaving the boat to drift back into the middle.

The sun is coming up. Ned swings his sack over his shoulder and starts walking, keeping as close to the river as he can. He sees a convict woman pissing in the woods and two soldiers playing dice on the back of a bullock cart. A farmer stops sawing logs to gaze at him and a shepherd's boy calls after him, but Ned doesn't stop.

After walking for an hour he slumps down on the grass. The sack is all wet and the cheese has crumbled to pieces and the bread is soggy, but Ned is so hungry he could eat anything.

A huge sawlog, as fat as a hogshead, floats down the middle of the river, bobbing in the current, dragging behind it smaller logs lashed in bundles and tied to the larger one with ropes. As the logs glide out of sight Ned thinks he hears the pup barking, but it's only a dog.

~

LIKE ANY diligent reader of the newspaper, Mrs Jakes knows the risks in straying outside the settlement. Every traveller who has ever been menaced by blacks, or waded through a swollen river, or been robbed of his belongings by bandits, makes a point of reporting it to the editor, Mr Bent, who publishes an account, suitably improved and embroidered, in the columns of the *Hobart Town Gazette*.

Mrs Jakes does not pass on these reports verbatim, but qualifies them with her own information, gleaned from casual encounters with soldiers, servants and tradesmen as well as other sources which she keeps to herself. She can cite the number of absconders at large on the island; the names, ages and physical descriptions of the principal bushrangers; the head of cattle speared north and south of the Jordan River in the past month; and the weight of beef delivered last week to the meat commissariat. She knows which rivers are up and which are down; where a bullock cart risks getting bogged on the road to Pitt Water; and how much ale is in the tap at the Catkins Hotel in Jericho. She can give a good description of the journey to Port Dalrymple without ever having ventured beyond the end of Macquarie Street. If there was such a thing as a gazetteer for travellers, Mrs Jakes would be it.

Mr Kidney is content to listen to her advice without entirely believing it. He suspects the newspaper of elaboration, if not fabrication, and he suspects his housekeeper of elaborating on those elaborations. He considers himself, in spite of evidence to the contrary, a worldly, practical man who does not need to be told how to look after himself.

Mrs Jakes is aware of certain distractions that might delay his return: farmers' wives prevailing on him to say grace over a plate of roast beef, convict shepherds cleansing their souls over a bottle of rum. She knows he will be more charitably received by the settlers in York Plains than by the insolent tradesmen and usurious shopkeepers in Hobart Town. She takes it for granted that, despite her careful instructions, the chaplain will get lost and have to rely on some farmer's boy to guide him home. For all these reasons, she knows not to expect him until she hears his horse trotting up the gravel path.

On this Saturday evening, Mrs Jakes is not worried. It's half past seven and drizzling and the chaplain (she thinks) will probably be settling in for the night in one of the farmhouses along the Jordan River. She will draw the curtains in the chaplain's study and place on his desk a letter which has arrived from the Bishop of Sydney. Perhaps she will leave a plate of cheese, or the remains of a cold fowl, on the off chance that he will stumble home late and want feeding. Or perhaps she won't. If he arrives after midnight, as he has been known to do, she will make it clear that she resents being dragged out of bed to let him in. Depending on his mood, and how drunk he is, the chaplain will either stand his ground and glower, or crawl away to his armchair and spend the night in his study, snoring and wheezing until she comes in the next morning and throws opens the windows.

Mrs Jakes has prepared a small supper for herself, a boiled egg and some hard biscuits. Her umbrella, mob-cap and shoes are in the hall, suggesting that she may, despite the inclement weather, be intending to go out later. She is about to rake the fire when she hears a sharp, presumptuous knock at the front door. She carries the poker to the window and squints through the curtains.

There are two women standing on the porch. One is Mrs Sweetwater. The other is her maidservant, a pretty Antrim woman with whom Mrs Jakes has sometimes exchanged a few words while queuing for bread. She puts down her poker and straightens her apron and opens the door.

'Good evening,' says Mrs Sweetwater, politely enough, lowering her umbrella and indicating her wish to come in.

'Good evening,' replies Mrs Jakes, not moving.

'Please inform Mr Kidney that I wish to speak with him.' She looks past Mrs Jakes down the narrow hallway, expecting Mr Kidney's head to emerge from his study.

'The chaplain is not at home.'

A sceptical pause. 'Indeed? But are you expecting him?'

'No.'

Mrs Sweetwater glances at her maidservant, who is staring at an improbably youthful portrait of the Reverend Mr Kidney on horseback, Bible in hand, conferring his blessings on an emaciated convict. The picture was painted in Bristol by his friend Mr Thomas Dudley, who died soon after from a fever. It was bequeathed to the chaplain and reached Hobart Town inside a consignment of spirits. Mr Kidney was pleased with the likeness and touched by the poignancy of the metaphor. He could not remember the act itself but persuaded himself that the artist had captured some essential inner truth. He considered the scene very lifelike and vigorous and hung it at once in the most prominent place he could think of, where it has amused his visitors ever since.

Mrs Sweetwater snaps her fingers irritably at the servant and says, 'I was under the impression his absence was to be brief.'

'It was to be as brief, madam, as the business it concerned.'

'Did not the unfortunate Mr Wheeler die on Monday?'

Mrs Jakes confirms this fact with a nod.

'And are you not concerned by the fact that today is Saturday?'

'I dare say there was enough to detain him.'

Mrs Sweetwater's eyes widen, lifting her small feathered

hat a fraction above her hairline. 'And pray what might this have entailed?'

'It is the chaplain's business, madam, and you will have to question him.' She starts to shut the door. 'I will tell him you called.'

'Wait!'

Mrs Jakes hesitates.

'Give him this.' She produces from the pocket of her coat a fragrant little parcel, wrapped in wax paper and tied with a black ribbon, one of several such parcels by which she persists in reminding Mr Kidney of her affections.

The housekeeper gazes at it distastefully, knowing that it contains snuff, which she detests, and that it will come with some compromising social obligation which the chaplain will find it difficult to refuse. She is fully aware of the warm relations that once existed between Mrs Sweetwater and Mr Kidney and has no wish to see them revived. On various occasions she has attempted to prevent the parcels from reaching their destination, but found Mrs Sweetwater's resourcefulness the equal of her own. Reluctantly, she agrees to deliver it. 'Is there a message?'

Mrs Sweetwater grimaces as if to say that, were there a message, she would not entrust a word of it to Mrs Jakes, then shoos her servant down the steps, hearing the door slam loudly behind her.

~

A Daring and bloody Attack was carried out on Thursday last at Mr JEMOTT's Farm near Lemon's Lagoon. On the Evening in question a

Party of Soldiers led by Lieutenant MURRAY called on Mr Jemott for a Supply of fresh Meat to be drawn on the Government. The Party was leaving when it was surprised by Bushrangers intent on stealing Tobacco. In the ensuing fierce Hostilities, the Soldiers were outfought and every Man disarmed, the only Inconvenience to the Bandits being a Flesh Wound inflicted on MICHAEL BRODIE. The Bushrangers then proceeded to strip the Soldiers of their Uniforms, which they brazenly exchanged for their own ragged Garments, there being much Dispute among the Bandits over who should imperson-ate the Officer. They left, with strict Admonitions that any Attempt to betray them would be repaid with Violence. The Victims were unable to free themselves and were only saved by the timely Intervention of a Neighbour, who came in Search of Sugar. The Bandits were not ashamed to boast of their Achievements, and told Mr Jemott they were the same that assaulted a Constable in Herdsman's Cove; stole Mr CAWSTON's Wethers; and burnt Col DAVEY's Haystacks.

~

OPENING ONE eye to the light, the Reverend Mr Kidney finds himself in a tent. It is a mystery to him how he got there and—since he cannot imagine entering of his own accord—who put him there. He opens his other eye and sees a pewter plate containing some bones and a portion of charred sheep's liver. His boots and breeches are in a heap, his fat pink legs covered by a blue woollen blanket. There are several empty bottles lying around him. His fowling piece is propped against the tent pole.

He manages, with some effort, to extricate himself from the blanket, turns around on his hands and knees to face the entrance, and crawls slowly towards it. Fumbling his way through the flap, he pokes his bald head out like a tortoise.

The sun is shining weakly through a thick morning mist. There's a knapsack on the grass, an empty port bottle, the creamy knuckle of a gnawed bacon bone. But the man who gnawed it is gone, so is his musket, and so are his companions.

The chaplain blinks, rubs his eyes, pulls his head in. His silver brandy flask is lying at the head of the empties, apparently the last to fall. He reaches for it, hoping that God—or somebody—might have seen fit to fill it while he slept. The crystal stopper is missing, its silver chain snapped off at the neck. The flask is empty. Mr Kidney sits for a while with his head in his hands before he becomes aware of a rustling outside the tent. He looks out and sees the corporal standing by the fire with his prick out, pissing on the embers. He sees the chaplain watching him but doesn't bother to turn away. There is a look on his face that betrays the amused recollection of some boorish humiliation inflicted on Mr Kidney that the victim himself can barely remember. The glistening parabola sags and falls. The corporal shakes his left boot, grins lewdly at the chaplain and wanders off without a word.

'Come back...wait,' shouts Mr Kidney. He scrambles

back inside, wrestles with his breeches, pulls on the wrong boot. 'Stay where you are...I will be out directly.' He crawls out of the tent, squinting at the sunshine, but the corporal has vanished. 'Don't leave me...come back...my horse...'

He is suddenly gripped by the need to empty his bladder. As he stands there splashing the tree, the night comes rushing back to him: the rum, the mutton burnt to cinders on the fire, drunken taunting with a bottle of port, a soldier's tunic nailed to a tree and blasted with buckshot. Shreds of scarlet cloth are embedded in the silver trunk like spots of blood.

Mr Kidney buttons up his breeches and waddles back to the tent. As he pulls at the flaps he hears something moving in the woods behind him. Looking up, he glimpses a dark shape, perhaps a man standing with his back to him. He calls out. The figure retreats further into the shadows. Mr Kidney reaches inside the tent for his fowling piece. 'Come out, sir, whoever you are. I can see you plainly. I will not be stalked.'

The stalker emerges indolently from the shadows, snorts and tugs at a clump of grass. It is Nelson, his piebald gelding, wearing a soft felt hat and with a belt of powder cartridges slung around its neck.

Mr Kidney puts down his gun. Looking around, he sees that the clearing is strewn with unmilitary objects: a bone-handled clothes brush; a miniature edition of Milton's sonnets, bound in green morocco, with the name 'Elizabeth Jemott' written inside; a gentleman's linen shirt; a bundle of ladies' silk handkerchiefs tied with ribbon; a jar of French mustard with its wax seal intact; a pair of steel-rimmed spectacles and a constable's truncheon.

The chaplain picks up everything except the truncheon, and places it, as if for safekeeping, between the roots of a tree. Then, on second thoughts, he removes the sonnets, pauses, holds up the linen shirt (which is far too small for him but might be cut up to form a summer vest), reconsiders the ladies' handkerchiefs, the clothes brush and the mustard, and finally stuffs everything into his satchel in the hope that Mrs Jakes will find some use for them.

Meanwhile the horse has wandered off another fifty yards, out of nothing but wilfulness and, perhaps, curiosity to see what the chaplain will do next.

Mr Kidney buckles his satchel and pulls it over his shoulder. He searches the shadows until he sees Nelson scratching his neck against a tree—an action which usually signals recalcitrance.

Had he been thirty years younger, he would simply have marched up to the animal and cuffed it into submission. Even ten years ago he would have been confident of cornering it and subduing its rebellious instincts. But years of wheedling and pandering to its whims have worn away any vestige of authority. The only tools he now has left are bribery and stealth.

The gelding stops scratching and eyes the chaplain coldly through the trees. It is no fool. It has seen things during the night (a sheep's carcass, a gentleman's wig left to rot in the river) that imply the presence of more dangerous creatures than Mr Kidney. The ruffians who put a hat on its head and a cartridge belt around its neck were notably grudging with their oats. In short, it seems better to remain with the chaplain than abandon him. The animal swishes its tail and, having made up its mind, trots towards him.

~

A sorry Tale has reached our Ears concerning the Begetters of the celebrated SOOTERKIN, or (as the Doubters have it) SEAL PUP, upon whose miraculous Conception we have already confided our Opinion. We are informed that the furry Infant was mislaid, presumed stolen, on Tuesday last, within Sight of the Barracks Gate. Further, that the Boy entrusted with chaperoning the Creature has also disappeared. Such, we may observe, is the Fickleness of FATE, which delivers new Riches into our Hands only to steal that Portion which is ours already.

~

A SMALL and sombre group of citizens has gathered around the dead gum tree opposite the shop of Messrs Lloyd and Lonsdale. No-one is speaking or looking anyone else in the eye, or acknowledging in any way whatsoever that they may be assembled here for the same purpose. But between the shifting of feet and the lighting of pipes and the jostling of umbrellas, you might catch some furtive glances directed at a small printed notice, partly obscured by a much larger one announcing the forced sale of a brewer's copper.

The smaller notice advertises a meeting to be held 'TONIGHT at 9 o'clock Prompt', where citizens interested in the recovery of the sooterkin, and the safe return of the boy, may subscribe to an expedition calculated to achieve both.

The notice is unsigned, but the artful tone and smudged print betray the authorship of Mr Bent, proprietor of the *Hobart Town Gazette*. The suddenness of the announcement and the extraordinary timing of the meeting on this wet and misty Saturday night are testament to Mr Bent's penchant for melodrama in commercial matters. It may be assumed that his motives on this occasion are not exclusively philanthropic.

It is past nine and a lantern is glowing in the window of Messrs Lloyd and Lonsdale's shop, where the bird-like figure of Mr Lonsdale can be seen putting the finishing touches to a display of possum hats that Mr Lloyd will almost certainly dismantle on Monday morning.

The light of the lantern is enough to identify the nearest member of the group as Mr Sculley. Next to him, pretending to adjust the hands of his pocket watch, is the well-upholstered form of Dr Benjamin Banes, whose ship, the *Seagull*, sailed this morning (as reported in the columns of the *Gazette*) for London, via Sydney. To Banes's left is the slight, restless figure of Mrs Fitzgerald, the schoolmistress. Some distance to her left, exuding an air of profound disagreeableness, is Mr Salter, the superintendent of government herds. The short, stout woman in the woollen cloak, standing a few feet apart from the others, is Mrs Jakes. A visible frostiness exists between the chaplain's housekeeper and the woman next to her, Mrs Sweetwater, whose umbrella seems to be inclined with the sole aim of directing a trickle of water down Mrs Jakes's back. It is clear that neither woman expected to find the other one here. Mrs Sweetwater's maid is self-consciously stationed at her mistress's elbow, pretending not to notice as Mr Lonsdale cheekily attempts to interest her in a possum hat.

At twenty minutes past nine Mr Bent arrives at a businesslike trot, his forehead streaked with printer's ink and the smell of whisky hanging on his breath. He has no umbrella. He stops on the other side of the road, nods to Mr Lonsdale, still arranging his possum hats, and assesses the effectiveness of his summons. He looks neither pleased nor disappointed, shrugs, plucks at the collar of his coat and slips a lozenge into his mouth.

Whatever Mr Bent has been doing, it has made him sweat. His ears are red and there are beads of perspiration on his temples. The rain has eased to a fine grey drizzle which turns to steam on his head, so that the printer appears to be walking in his own personal miasma. 'I was delayed,' he says, offering no further explanation.

A heavy cotton apron protrudes six inches below the hem of his coat, a sort of gutter from which a stream of inky droplets splashes at his feet. He identifies those present, hesitating before putting a name to the Harvard surgeon.

It is Mr Bent's intention to dispatch, under the banner of his public-spirited journal, a small expedition to trace the whereabouts of the so-called sooterkin—he smiles mischievously at Mr Sculley—or seal pup, to ascertain whether it is alive or dead, injured or in good health, what tricks it has learnt and—arching his eyebrows at the schoolmistress—whether it has acquired any semblance of language; in short to find out everything that can be found out for a sum not exceeding two guineas per diem, payable in arrears, upon production of receipts.

Whether the scheme might have been induced by a steep

drop in the circulation of the *Gazette*, brought about by the rise in its cover price from sevenpence-halfpenny to ninepence, is open to speculation. Mr Bent's conscience on this matter, as on all matters, is clear. But to impress upon his audience the altruistic spirit of the enterprise, he holds up a promissory note (which happens to be made out to himself) for the sum of two guineas.

'What about the boy?' asks Mrs Jakes, since nobody else will ask.

Mr Bent slips the note back in his pocket. The *Hobart Town Gazette* has recorded the fates of numerous children who have drowned or starved to death or been found murdered in the woods. 'Of course,' he says, 'we are concerned to find the boy, if it's not too late.'

'And the mother?' inquires Mrs Fitzgerald.

'Distraught, ma'am. A mere ghost, by all accounts.'

'The fa—'

'A drunkard.'

'A sad story,' remarks the schoolmistress.

'Almost a tragedy, ma'am. I dare say it will merit some further paragraphs in due course.'

'Is it true,' asks Mr Sculley, 'that an effort to sell the sooterkin was made on the morning after its disappearance?'

'I have heard that rumour, sir,' says the printer, 'but verification is not possible since the creature itself was never produced. More curiosities are offered for sale on the wharves than will ever see the light of day. Ladies and gentlemen, it is my belief that the sooterkin, if that's what we are to call it, is not more than twenty miles from this settlement, and will be ransomed in due course.'

'A kidnapping?'

'That, Mr Salter, is my considered opinion.'

'Then shall we not wait to be informed of it?'

'Perhaps the villain cannot write,' remarks Mrs Fitzgerald.

'Perhaps,' observes Banes, 'it ain't been kidnapped at all.'

This remark is met with impatient looks and a growl from the herdsman.

'Would you care to elaborate on that hypothesis, sir?'

Banes waits for the murmuring to die down. 'There is a profit to be had from the crittur. The smell of money does bitter things to a man that don't possess it. My guess is the varmint has been shipped away to frustrate the ambitions of a better man.'

'You are marvellously perceptive, sir, of the abductor's motive. You appear to read his thoughts.'

Banes is conscious of having said too much. 'I know malice, Mr Bent. I mean, I have seen it. I believe the act was done out of malice.'

A half smile passes over the printer's face, as if to advise the American that his discomfiture has been noted and filed away for future reference in his columns. 'And what if I was to inform you, sir, that not a single vessel has departed the settlement since the creature was stolen—except, of course, your own—and that the logical course is therefore to search for it here.'

'In that case, Bent, I say your two guineas per diem is hardly enough to keep four men in liquor and tobacco.'

'You misunderstand the *Gazette*'s offer. It is not to be spent on liquor, sir, but on expenses necessary to the object of the expedition—by which I mean the recovery of the sooterkin.'

'Then you will pay for the pelt?'

'It must be alive, Mr Banes. It will serve no purpose to find a carcass. The *Gazette* will not pay to see the creature dead.'

'And the boy?' demands Mrs Jakes.

'Ma'am, we are anxious to find them both.'

There is a long pause, during which several of the gentlemen indicate their willingness to embark on such an expedition. Finally Mrs Sweetwater says, 'You have not ventured two guineas to find the chaplain.'

'Two guineas, ma'am, would not begin to register our high opinion of the chaplain'—reaching for a lozenge—'but nor, we believe, would it hasten his return.'

Mrs Jakes shoots an angry look at the printer that momentarily displaces the frown trained on Mrs Sweetwater. She knows that Mr Bent is no admirer of the chaplain. She has read the scurrilous items in his columns: wry allusions to his health, insinuations of drunkenness, disparaging accounts of his sermons. She wishes the printer to be aware that, were the chaplain to come to any harm, the slights against him would not be forgotten or forgiven. These points having—at least in Mrs Jakes's opinion—been made and understood, she delivers a final withering gaze at Mrs Sweetwater and shuffles off into the darkness, leaving the expeditioners to disperse.

~

The Gazette is pleased to inform the Public that an Expedition has been undertaken by some leading Citizens of this Town, to discover the Fate of the Seal Baby, or SOOTERKIN, and his Human Sibling. The Party set out at 9 o'clock on Sunday Morning, resolving also to make Enquiries into the Whereabouts of Mr KIDNEY, whose Safety, as a Minister of the Anglican Church, can scarcely be doubted, but whose Comfort may be presumed to be much diminished by his prolonged Absence from Society. The Members of the Party, having no Wish for premature Celebration, desired no Farewell, but will be glad to receive appropriate Tidings at this Office, to be forwarded by the Printer at his own expense, when the Opportunity permits.

PS. As Human Ingenuity is no respecter of weekly Deadlines, Readers are advised that a daily Bulletin will be posted at this Office, Copies of which may be had for ONE PENNY, to be paid upon Collection.

~

NED WANDERS for two days and nights, with nothing to eat but a bacon bone he stole from a farmer's kitchen and only haystacks and barns to sleep in. He leaves the path beside the River Derwent at New Norfolk and follows a track over the Jordan River to Bagdad where he meets a grog-seller who takes him as far as Muddy Plains. He doesn't know where he's going, only that now he's started he mustn't stop. He doesn't know who he's looking for, but asks everyone he meets if they have set eyes on a weasel-faced man with a baggage under his arm.

The farmers' boys are all ribs and ears, like their dogs. Some say they have but can't remember when, and others say they haven't but so-and-so saw him, and the man was riding by the river on a black mare, or loitering in the woods on a grey one, and had a scar under his ear, or blood on his shoes, or an empty sleeve for an arm.

On Monday morning he spots a dark thing floating in the reeds on the far bank of the Coal River. The river is not wide but there is no bridge and the current is too fast to swim. Ned walks another quarter of a mile to where the river veers to the left. Just around the bend he finds a willow tree blown down by a storm, with a smaller tree caught up in its roots. The branches are knotted together in a lattice, allowing Ned to clamber across.

At first glance it looks like a drowned man lying face down in the water. But as Ned pokes at it with a stick the thing comes loose and floats towards him and he realises it is a black calf, speared and thrown in the river. Most of its underside has been eaten away and its entrails are tumbling out. Ned pushes it away in disgust. As he scrambles back up the bank, he hears a loud splash. He looks up and sees a boy standing there. The boy is smaller than Ned, about six years old, with a bald patch on the side of his head, like a horse that has rubbed itself raw on a post.

'It's mine,' he says.

'What is?'

'That,' says the boy. 'I found it.'

Ned looks back at the calf turning slowly in the current. 'It's dead.'

'Don't care,' says the boy. 'It's mine.' He lifts his hand

to throw another stone, but hesitates when Ned picks up a bigger one. For a moment he doesn't know what to do, but stands there pouting and swaying and scratching his bald patch. Then he drops the stone and says, 'The man said I could have it.'

'What man?'

'A man. He was lost. I showed him the path and he said I could have it.'

Ned hazards a description of the stranger who came to supper. 'Was that him?'

'Maybe.'

'Which way did he go?'

The boy points vaguely behind him.

'Did he have a bundle?'

'Maybe.'

The rotting carcass has floated a hundred yards down-river and snagged on the roots of a tree. 'There,' says Ned. 'You can have it.'

The boy doesn't move or speak; he merely pouts. When Ned looks back at him, he's still pouting.

A mile further on the path swings around and starts heading away from the river. There are some sheep in the paddocks but no cattle and no farmhouses, only convict shepherds' huts with bark roofs and a flap of cowhide for a window and smoke puffing out of crooked mud chimneys. Ned has heard tales of what convicts do to boys they catch hold of, so he keeps his distance. A boy was dug up dead in Riley's Woods last year, with nothing on him but a pair of kangaroo slippers. They never proved who did it, but people said his neck was wrung by a shepherd, the same as happened to a black child the month before, and when the shepherd was found cut to pieces with an axe nobody lifted a hand to bury him.

By now it's starting to get dark. Somewhere in the hills ahead Ned hears devils caterwauling. He watches a hawk hover in the wind before plummeting to earth and snatching something out of the grass.

The sun is almost down when he comes across a little cottage hidden among the trees—a rough timber building with a wide verandah and a shingle roof. There is a small stables at the back and a potato cart in the paddock. The fences are strung with dead magpies and strips of sacking. A she-goat is tied to a post and half a dozen sheep are moving about anxiously in the gloom.

Creeping closer, Ned notices that the door to the cottage is ajar. A thin sliver of light is shining across the verandah. He watches smoke curling from the chimney before the breeze shrugs it away.

Someone has stacked a pile of firewood behind the stables. Ned crouches out of sight and tosses a small pebble onto the roof. The pebble clatters noisily onto the verandah. Ned waits for somebody to come out but nobody does. He throws another, then crawls close enough to peer through the crack in the doorway.

He pushes the door open a few more inches and pokes his head inside. There is no-one at home but a rusty oil lamp is hanging from the rafters. The floor is bare and badly joined, so the wind blows up through the boards. On one side of the room is a table and chair and on the other a narrow plank bed covered with possum blankets. There's a wooden cot next to the window and some faded needlework on the wall and an iron stove and a bowl of feathers and a switch broom and a spinning wheel with spokes missing.

Someone has left a meal uneaten on the table: bread and cheese, salt pork, pickled onions, sheep's brains, capers, cabbage, quince jelly and raisins. Ned has never seen such a feast before, all laid out in tiny portions, as if the person who left it enjoyed eating but had no appetite. He quickly polishes off the bread and pork and washes them down with a mug of wine. Then he takes a fancy to the cheese and slips that in his pocket. He tries a pickled onion and makes up his mind to take a few of them too. After that it's the capers and raisins. Finally there's nothing left on the table except cabbage and sheep's brains. Ned is disposed to leave these, so the owner will not go hungry. But he sticks his finger in the brains just in case and finds they go very nicely with a spoonful of quince jelly. He is now so groggy from the wine that he can hardly stand. So he sits down on the bed to gather his thoughts and decides it wouldn't harm him to lay his head on the pillow for a minute or two and before long he's fast asleep.

~

SARAH DYER sits on her straight-backed chair spinning out her sorrow like a spider. She weaves it tighter and tighter, whimpering softly as she mourns the loss of her children. William blunders into it, bleary-eyed, pockets empty, wallowing in beer and self-pity.

'What is it, woman?' he says, swaying on his bony stilts. 'Is it me that took 'im?'

She glares at him bitterly but won't answer.

Dyer squirms out of her gaze and throws a parcel of oysters down on the table, next to another that has not been touched. 'Will you starve yourself to death?'

At night she weeps out loud.

Everywhere he looks, Dyer sees the stranger's ugly face sneering at him. It smirks from the bottom of a pot of ale. It lurks in his oysters and hangs, grinning, in his tobacco smoke. It's there when he goes to sleep and when he wakes up. It's a torment worse than cramps and colic, worse than the pox and the pox doctor, worse than boils and blisters and buboes. It's a torment, thinks Dyer, that must be got rid of, or suffered for ever.

~

IT STARTLES Mr Kidney to find that one hill can look so much like another. Or that a creek can exist one minute and vanish the next. Or that a mountain can change shape while you look at it. Such observations fly in the face of what had, until now, seemed the guiding principle of creation: that nature was an impassive creature, prone to violent eruptions and earthquakes, but on the whole respectful of the superior wit of man—represented, in this case, by himself. It dawns on him now that nature, for all its grandeur, is not above the sort of trickery practised by quacks and cardsharps.

For all this the chaplain feels strangely contented, having convinced himself—in the absence of any dissenting voice—that it was he who banished the soldiers from his presence and not they who abandoned him. The gentle undulations of his horse incline him to believe that the animal has finally embraced its subservient role. The only thing disturbing his tranquillity is the knowledge that he has nothing more appetising to eat than a handful of Mrs Jakes's stale biscuits. He has not given up hope of seeing Mr Edward Lord clattering towards him with his saddlebags full of smoked ham and mustard. Or of stumbling by chance upon a party of picnickers with their hampers just opened. Either would go some way to restoring his faith in a God whose behaviour has become ineffably mysterious, not to say capricious.

The infant, for instance, which the common people saw fit to liken to a seal pup and which did indeed look identical to that animal, now seems to Mr Kidney to be more in the nature of a theological puzzle than a miracle. Not that he is blind to the possibility of the birth being—as several ladies have privately assured him—fraudulently conceived. But were similar aspersions not cast on the two-legged pony? And had that unfortunate beast not rebuffed its detractors, and shown by its courageous fight for life the very spirit and struggle which is proof of divine inspiration? The seal pup is, he concedes, a more ambivalent proposition in which commerce has played an unseemly part. But since when has holiness been an obstacle to profit (except in his own case)?

Mr Kidney has always resisted the worldly argument that the Almighty's approval can be calculated in riches, happiness, health or any other measure of material satisfaction. He has struggled to find sanctuary in his books, in the company of his friends, even in the staunch but wordless loyalty of Mrs Jakes. His faith has wavered and weakened but never collapsed. Nevertheless, a benign Creator could hardly fail to notice that his mounting debts, and diminishing ability to repay them, have done nothing to enhance his authority in the eyes of an indifferent congregation, and that his brittle health has made him the victim of malicious innuendo that can only make his vocation harder.

Mr Kidney's thoughts go round and round, visiting old haunts, nodding at familiar platitudes, pausing to wrestle with conundrums to which he has never yet found the answer, and finally emerging no wiser than when they began.

He pulls up his horse beside a huge dishevelled gum which looks very much like a tree he passed several hours earlier and had the foresight to mark with a blank page of his prayer book, in case he happened to pass it again. The page has fallen off and is lying among the leaf litter, where an army of ants is attempting to drag it away. Impaling it on a stick, the chaplain feels oddly proud of himself, as if the stratagem proved his competence as a navigator, rather than the reverse.

The gum tree is at the crossroads of two narrow paths, neither of which extends more than a hundred yards before losing itself in the bushes. The smaller of the two gives some impression of having been travelled quite recently by a man in a dog cart.

The wooded grassland is crisscrossed with paths, most of them trodden out by convict stockmen and shepherds moving east along the corridor between the Coal River and the coast at Grindstone Bay.

The chaplain, flapping at flies with his handkerchief, hears a noise in the bushes to his left. He turns in his saddle as a wallaby leaps from the scrub and bounds away among the straggly trees.

His horse snorts and swings its head while Mr Kidney

tries to identify the most promising path. He looks again at the ruts (the tracks of a wheelbarrow, requisitioned and later abandoned by the deputy surveyor during a tour of the district) and, after some hapless observations of the sun, decides to follow them. The horse breaks into a trot for a minute or two before reverting to its customary shambling walk.

The rotten warmth of the woods makes the chaplain drowsy. The afternoon sun squeezes out fat beads of sweat which slide down his temples and roll like marbles around the folds of his neck before scuttling down his back. His smooth bald head lolls on his shoulder, then snaps upright, then lolls back. His mouth opens in a flatulent yawn. The steady jolt of the horse works its way through the blubbery mass of his legs and into his stomach and up through his multiplicity of chins as far as his eyelids, which sag lower and lower, until they're hardly open at all, and his fingers loosen their grip on the reins and he's asleep.

~

It is with no Satisfaction, and some Bewilderment, that we report the latest Twist in the Tale of the Seal Child. We are informed that the Father of the Infant, whether out of Sorrow or Confusion, has himself disappeared, leaving the distressed Mother alone with her Grief, to lament the Loss of Family and Fortune.

~

DURING THE night Ned dreams that his spirit flies right out of him and goes looking for Arthur. It soars over mountains and glides over forests and searches under rocks and behind waterfalls but can find no trace of the pup. He wakes up snivelling. He has the sense of having committed a terrible crime without knowing what it was. The door is not where he remembers it. The window is gone and everything is back to front, as if somebody moved the bed while he slept. There is a pair of moleskin trousers hanging from a nail above him which was not there when he went to sleep. For a moment he thinks he sees the pup's whiskery chin poking out. He leaps up but finds only the frayed threads of an old sock. Big hot tears well up and tumble down his cheeks.

He wipes his face on his sleeve and tries to remember where he is. The room is dark and musty. His sack is under the table where he dropped it. There's a smoky smell from the oil lamp. He remembers the sheep's brains and the wine and sitting down on the bed, but nothing after that. The cabbage he left on the table is gone. He sees now that there is a window, but someone has hung a blanket over it.

As he gazes up at the blanket, Ned hears a sound like an animal turning over on its straw. Then a groan and the smack of wet lips. The hairs on his neck stand up. There is someone else in the room.

He holds his breath and listens. Whoever it is is fast asleep. Ned is almost too scared to move. He swings his legs gently over the edge and feels for the floor with his toes but someone has left a mug on the floor and over it goes with a crash. A voice says, 'What is your name?'

Ned doesn't know whether to bolt at once for the door or stay and bluff his way out.

'Your name, boy?' says the voice again. 'You are a boy, I suppose?'

It sounds deeper than a woman's voice but not so deep as a man's. 'Ned,' he answers, taking a step closer to the door.

'You're welcome to go,' says the voice, 'only you'll please leave the raisins, if they are not eaten already.'

Ned looks down at the mound of blankets that appears to contain the voice. 'I ate some,' he says.

'I thought so,' says the voice. 'I never met a boy that didn't steal raisins when he got the chance.'

It seems to Ned that the voice is not very menacing after all. 'Eating ain't the same as stealing,' he says.

The voice grunts but says nothing, and for a moment Ned thinks it has gone back to sleep. But then it asks, 'Why are you running away, Ned?'

'I'm not.'

'You are too sallow for a shepherd's boy.'

'That's because I ain't one.'

'Then what are you?'

Ned searches for a face among the blankets but cannot decide which end is which. He opens the door a fraction to allow a bar of sunshine into the room. Now he can discern a pair of small leathery feet and two scaly ankles webbed with blue veins. A breeze blows through the open door and the feet withdraw quickly under the blankets.

Finally Ned says, 'I'm looking for someone.'

There's a grunt from the blankets and a heave and a yawn and an old woman's wrinkled hand gropes along the edge of the table for a pair of wire spectacles. Her bony fingers curl around the spectacles and she raises her head a few inches off the pillow and perches the spectacles on her nose. There is a broken teacup on the table with a saucer upside down on it. The old woman carefully removes the saucer and lifts the teacup to her mouth. Ned sees her thin lips twitching. She takes a small swig and then puts it down, leaving a milky moustache over the real one. Then she licks her lips and rattles the teacup down on the saucer. Her wheezing grows softer until Ned can scarcely hear her breathing at all.

'I never heard of a mortal soul that wasn't looking for someone or something,' she says. 'Who are you looking for, Ned?'

'I'm looking for the man that stole Arthur.'

'Arthur being who, if you please?'

Ned recites the story of Arthur's arrival exactly as the newspaper had it, but with a few words left out and some added about Mr Trelawny and his instruments. The old woman nods to herself and murmurs something under her breath. Then Ned tells her about the stranger who came to supper and how Arthur was stolen and his mam with her arms and legs wrapped around him like an octopus and his pa drunk and how he crept out of the house before dawn and the dead calf in the river and what the boy with the stones told him. 'I must find Arthur,' he says at last, 'else I can't go home.'

She nods again and turns over so Ned can see her properly. Her face is loose and wrinkled, like an apple that has gone soft. She has a small crumpled nose but her gaze is hard and knotty. Ned thinks she must be as old as Methuselah, or older. She allows him to stare for a while and says, 'Have you never laid eyes on a witch before, boy?'

'There's no such women as witches,' says Ned.

She smiles and plucks an eyelash. 'Isn't there, now?'

'No, ma'am,' says Ned. Then he asks, 'Are you a witch?'

'I'm a widow, boy, with no children to look after, which is as lonely as a witch.'

Ned glances behind him at the wooden cot painted with rabbits, but before he can speak the old woman folds back her blankets and says, 'A gentleman came by here two days ago, which gentleman might be the one you're looking for, and might not. His horse was all worn out and he wanted mine, which I wouldn't give him.'

Ned asks if the man had a bundle with him, or a box, or anything that twitched under his coat.

'Maybe he kept it hidden,' she says. 'He was a sly one all right.'

'Did he have a hat?' asks Ned.

'Is that what it was?' she asks. 'I never saw one like it before, except on the Scilly Islands, where all the harbour-men wear 'em.'

'It's him,' says Ned.

'Maybe it is,' says the old woman. She picks up the broken teacup and hands it to Ned. 'Goat's milk, Ned. It'll do you good.'

Ned can see at once that the milk is curdled and pulls away from it.

'You ain't sick are you, boy?'

'No, ma'am.'

'You look dropsical.'

'No, ma'am, I never dropped a thing.'

'You ain't got the fever?'

'No.'

'You never had the goiter?'

'No, ma'am.'

She drinks off the last of the milk and puts the cup back on its saucer. 'What about the gripe?'

Ned insists there's nothing wrong with him except the sheep's brains disagreed with him and he needs a shit. The old woman follows him to the door and watches as he wanders into the woods.

While squatting among the bushes, he sees her walk around the cottage twice, throw a basket of cabbage scraps to the sheep, and bend down to examine some marks on the ground.

Counting back the days, Ned realises that today is Tuesday. It's a week since the pup was taken. He remembers something Mr Goldfarb once told him, about setting a thief to catch a thief. He decides he must steal a horse. As the only horse he can see is the old woman's, it must be hers.

~

A Saddlebag has been found near the Banks of the Coal River, which we have Reason to believe is the Property of the REVEREND Mr KIDNEY, whose Whereabouts are still unknown.

~

SLUMPED IN his saddle, like a black wax figure melting in the sun, Mr Kidney doesn't notice his horse leave the path and sniff its way to a gorge, where it begins chewing on a clump of succulent grass.

Now and then the chaplain twitches, lifts his head a fraction, grunts and wraps his arms around the horse's neck, lulled by the bobbing of its head and the grind of its jaws and the squittering of its insides.

You might imagine, from the contented expression on his face, that Mr Kidney's dreams had ridden ahead, and were now cantering through country not unlike his native Oxfordshire which would (in due course, and after the usual convivial distractions) deliver him straight to the landing of the Derwent ferry. The ferryman, a rough but genial fellow with a fondness for clergymen, would be waiting to take him across the river, refusing all offers of payment, and perhaps even requesting the honour of accompanying him down Elizabeth Street, at least as far as the bridge, where Mr Kidney would be obliged to dismount in order to offer his hand to the crowd now applauding his safe return. Mrs Jakes would not be among them but, by the uncanny gift she has of anticipating when he is about to walk through the door, she would have a large roasted fowl waiting for him on the table, with hot brown gravy and an abundance of vegetables, and a bottle of claret which, for once, she would allow him to pour himself.

This is the sort of direction in which Mr Kidney's mind is accustomed to wander when left to itself.

But a closer look might suggest that his expression is less contented than perplexed. The chaplain's thoughts, far from returning him in triumph to Hobart Town, have turned around and are gingerly picking their way through the circumstances that brought him here, taunted by a monstrosity that science and the Bible have been unable to explain.

Somewhere along the path Mr Kidney catches a glimpse
of the two-legged pony born to Mr Galloway's grey mare,
which he never saw but read about in the newspaper. The
image of the pony grows clearer and clearer until the chaplain realises that he is riding it, perched on the creature's
pitiful spine, struggling to hold on while it trots on the furry
stumps of its missing limbs. He tries to jerk the beast to a
halt but the pony ignores his commands and even attempts
a short gallop before collapsing under him. The chaplain
looks about but doesn't recognise the country. Its features
seem simultaneously strange and familiar: twisted willows
along a river bank, a comb of yellow poplars leading
nowhere, a skeletal oak standing alone in a field.

Suddenly a figure appears. It is Mrs Jakes, on her knees,
scooping at the earth with a trowel. Beside her is a parcel the
size of a cauliflower, wrapped in a white rag. A private burial.

Once, many years ago, the chaplain watched from his
bedroom window while Mrs Jakes crouched over a freshly
dug hole beneath the she-oak in the corner of the garden.
He didn't ask what she was doing and she never said. But
a poor demented convict woman came to him shortly after-
wards begging forgiveness for the murder of a baby that
no living soul had ever seen.

The oak tree. Somewhere in the chaplain's study, tucked
away among his papers, or folded between the mildew-
spotted pages of a book, is a cutting from a government
gazette:

> A Quantity of very fine Acorns being saved from
> the Oaks in the Government Garden at Sydney,
> and brought to this Colony aboard the JUPITER,

Individuals desirous of cultivating that valuable
Timber will send their Names to the Secretary's
Office; when the Gardener will have Instructions
to supply those who may be Approved.

Seventeen of the Sydney acorns were given to the chaplain, who planted them as far afield as Pitt Water and New
Norfolk, where they either took to the dark soil, or didn't.
Of the seventeen acorns, eleven produced seedlings and
nine were robust enough to encourage hopes they would
reach maturity and drop acorns of their own, so that the
Reverend Mr Kidney's legacy could be celebrated in oak,
if nothing else.

It was a source of no small gratification to him that not
a single acorn entrusted to others sprouted, despite the
attention lavished on them by such dedicated horticultur-
alists as Mr Birch, the whale baron, and Mr Mossop, the
harbourmaster.

Surely God had played some small part in that success.
In any case, Mr Kidney took the precaution of inserting
the Almighty's name above his own on the brass plaques
that christened each trunk, in ornate lettering that was
conspicuously harder to decipher than the plain capitals of
'THOS KIDNEY'.

'Yours is it, sir? The trunk. Mr Kidney is it?' He is standing under an umbrella outside a coaching inn, eleven miles
from Bristol, gazing at the vehicle which is meant to replace
the one in which he was travelling, and travelling comfortably, until it slid into a ditch and broke its axle.

Behind him an old man, his jaw grotesquely deformed
by a tumour, the rest of him held together with a length of

rope around his middle, is heaving the black leather handle of a wooden trunk with the name 'THOS KIDNEY' engraved on a steel plate.

Inside the trunk is the sum total of his worldly possessions, except for some small articles of furniture left to the care of a remover, with orders to have it in Bristol no later than a fortnight before sailing. The trunk is stuffed almost to bursting with books and linen and shoes and china, so heavy that three men were hardly able to hoist it on to the roof of the coach. Which is very likely why it overturned, and the roof caved in.

The Reverend Mr Kidney, preparing to entrust himself to an uncertain future as chaplain of Van Diemen's Land and sensing that this has been a less than auspicious start, glances at the passengers staring at him balefully through the window of a private lounge. A flagon of port has been put at their disposal and several of the gentlemen have worked up fierce tempers, expressed in vengeful looks and sarcastic gestures. The ladies seem torn between pity and contempt. His own gaze is drawn to the flagon, and the untouched glass beside it, which was presumably intended for him.

'Your trunk is it, sir?' The old man, who could be packed inside the trunk with room to spare, rubs the steel plate with the sleeve of his coat, as if the sight of his name— 'THOS KIDNEY'—glinting in the candlelight will jog the chaplain's memory.

There were so many things he couldn't bring with him, things which would have lent a modicum of comfort to his spartan existence and eased the muddy misery of his first year. Books mostly, but also a green velvet smoking coat, some leather slippers, a polished steel shaving mirror and a set of ivory-handled brushes. And a violin, for which he had no talent, but whose loss seemed to symbolise some profound regression from cultivated English clergyman to mendicant colonial parson.

Gradually the chaplain becomes aware of a noise, the insistent yelp of a young seal. Then another. Then a third, a fourth. Sooterkins, barking in his ear, nuzzling him with their sharp whiskers. Sooterkins everywhere, wrinkling their black button noses, waiting to be baptised. The Reverend Mr Kidney is splashing water on their foreheads and blessing them one by one in the name of the Father, and the Son, and the Holy Ghost.

The horse lurches back, shaking the chaplain out of his dream and splattering his stockings with mud. A plump black lizard scampers away and squeezes itself under a rock. And Mr Kidney finds himself staring down the barrel of a cocked pistol.

~

IN A small stone cottage a hundred yards from the gaol, Mr Bent puts the final touches to his first bulletin. The iron printing press stands in the middle of the room, an oily, bow-legged thing, bolted to the wooden floor like a great black crab.

Sitting in the corner is the messenger who brought news of the expedition, a red-faced farmer's boy too bewitched by the machine to accept Bent's offer of sixpence for a bed in a boarding house. The boy, having been entrusted with the letter at a drinking trough three miles from Herdsman's

Cove, and walked all afternoon to deliver it, is now holding the scruffy document reverently in his lap.

The printer has been up all night leading his columns, trimming his margins, hyphenating and capitalising, greasing his gears and plunging himself up to the wrists in black ink in the cause of laying before the public the following penny pamphlet:

We are now in receipt of the first Communication from the Party in Search of the Sooterkin and are pleased to present the same to our Readers, exactly as it was conveyed to the Printer, without a Word added, nor subtracted, except in the Cause of Clarity:

'On Sunday Night, or rather at an early Hour Monday Morning, we came upon our first Clue to the Whereabouts of the Creature adjudged by some to be a Sooterkin, and by others a Seal Pup. We had lately enjoyed Supper at the Cat and Fiddle Hotel in Herdsman's Cove, and were preparing for Bed, when Mrs Fitzgerald, from her Room upstairs, noticed a Light upon a nearby Hill which, according to the Landlord, had not been there previously. (There being no Road or Habitation in that Direction.) Mr Sculley likewise observed the Light from an upper Window, and prevailed upon the Landlord to have his Servant ride out as far as the Stockyard, in the Hope of discerning the Cause of the Phenomenon.

'In the Meantime, Mr Salter and Dr Banes proceeded to arm themselves with the bold Intention of confronting the Illumination. Accordingly a Dog Cart was brought out, and two Horses harnessed, during which Operation the Light burned undimmed, and appeared to oscillate, as though suspended, and subject to the Vicissitudes of the Wind.

'The Landlord then recalled his Servant, and insisted on conveying the whole Party by Dray, with himself at the Reins, and as many Wolf-hounds as could be roused from their Sleep. The Ground being soft, and our Progress arduous, we were soon abandoned by the Dogs, who found livelier Subjects to distract them.

'Mr Salter was first to alight from the Vehicle, and signalled his Arrival with a Gunshot, the Effect of which was suddenly to extinguish the Illumination, and terminate all Hopes of an Encounter. Mr Sculley and Dr Banes searched in vain, and were disposed to declare the Expedition ended, when Mrs Fitzgerald happened upon a Copper Lamp, and the still-warm Embers of a Fire, among which lay the Remains of numerous Fishes and Shell-fish, recently consumed, and the Skeleton of an Animal bearing a tolerable Likeness to a Seal Pup.

'It being, in the Opinion of Mr Sculley, impossible to attempt an Identification of the Animal without the proper Instruments (though Mrs Fitzgerald thought it a Common Cat), we directed the Landlord's Man to collect the Bones, whereupon Mr Salter discovered a Quantity of Oats among the Bushes, and the Tracks of a Horse. Mrs Fitzgerald was resolved to pursue the Absconder at once, but after Contemplation of the Dangers of such a Course, was persuaded to wait until Morning.

'The Weather, however, deteriorated and when we returned after Breakfast, all Trace of them was erased. Upon enquiring at a nearby Farm, we learned that a peculiar Gentleman had requested Straw, and also a Quantity of Milk, with which he proposed to nourish his Whelp, whose Whereabouts he could not be pressed to reveal. He requested also a Basin and Soap and confessed himself needful of a Shave, though there was but a Day's Growth visible on his Chin. The Gentleman bore a Cicatrice on his Throat and appeared to be somewhat embarrassed for Money, as he could not pay for the Provisions he sought, but told the Farmer he had been inconvenienced by a Sickness in the Whelp, which had kept him from his Business.

'We are now strenuously engaged in the Pursuit of this Gentleman, whose strange Behaviour appears to implicate him in this Mystery.'

~

IT'S A princely shit and affords Ned plenty of time to invent a plan while the old woman goes about her business.

By the time he's finished, Ned has what he considers a very clever scheme in his head: he will tell the old woman he is sick after all, and stay in bed while she does her work, and promise to keep the fire going and anything else he can think of, and when she's gone he will break into the stables and saddle the horse and be gone before she returns.

Ned hurries back, stuffing his shirt tails into his breeches and slapping himself for not hitting upon the idea before.

The old woman comes out to meet him. She doesn't say anything but presses a scrap of cambric and some tallow soap into his hand and points towards a tree where a canvas washbasin is hung between two branches.

Ned reckons now that he has her measure and tells her

she can keep her soap (if it pleases her) as he did not shit upon his hands. But the widow answers that it is not Ned's hands that are covered in filth but his face and especially his vulgar tongue, and if he intends to have breakfast they will both need scrubbing. Ned folds his arms and frowns. He has a good mind to refuse but thinks better of it and takes the soap and scours his cheeks until they sting.

'You may call me Mrs Slade,' says the old woman, taking back the soap and scratching it with her thumbnail, as if to make sure his dirt has not stuck to it.

'You may call me Ned,' he answers, forgetting that he has already told her his name, and wishing he could have thought of some other name to give her now that he has made up his mind to steal her horse.

'Ned is what I have been calling you,' she says, and wanders back indoors.

Ned realises that he will need to give some evidence of being sick if the old woman is to believe him. He notices the bar of soap left on the verandah. He knows that convicts make themselves sick by eating soap and decides that by licking it he can make himself a little bit sick—sick enough to be left alone while the widow goes looking for her sheep.

He has hardly put his tongue to it when his belly starts churning and his mouth fills with froth and Mrs Slade, as he is now required to call her, is plunging him head first into a bucket of cold water.

By the time Ned has recovered she is sitting in her wicker chair, picking at a bowl of raisins in her lap. Her face is pinched in a mischievous grin. 'I heard of boys getting sick so they didn't have to wash,' she says, 'but I never heard of a boy washing so he could get sick.'

Ned holds his tongue.

'Well, Master Ned,' she says, blowing the dust off another raisin, 'I dare say there is something behind it.' She rolls it admiringly in her bony fingers before popping it in her mouth. 'No doubt you had a mind to steal my horse.'

Ned purses his lips so as not to betray himself. He listens to her grinding the seeds between her teeth and wonders if she is a witch after all.

'Believe me, Ned,' she says, 'I've not lived to be as old as I am to have my horse stolen by the likes of you.'

'Ain't you afraid of savages?' he asks, hoping to shake her out of her humour. 'Or bushrangers?'

The widow merely laughs, or rather cackles, and says she is on very lukewarm terms with both the bandits and the blacks and has never done any harm to them, nor received any either. Then she puts the bowl back on the table and drapes a cloth over it, as if she has a whim to make it disappear. But she reads his thoughts again and says it is only to keep the flies off.

'Why, Ned,' she says mockingly, 'are you afraid of 'em?'

'No, ma'am,' he answers. 'I ain't afraid.' There is a quaver in his voice. His lower lip trembles and suddenly Ned bursts into tears. The widow nods her wrinkled old head as if she saw the whole thing coming. She wipes her mouth on her apron and stands up. 'I dare say the thief will not get far without a fresh horse, or resting the one he's got, in which case we may run him down in a day or two if we are lucky.' She fetches the musket off the wall and pushes it into his hands. 'If I am not mistook, Ned, the fellow hid a pistol in his coat.'

'THANK GOD, sir,' exclaims the chaplain, resisting the temptation to throw out his right hand and reach for a heavenly handshake. 'You have found me.'

The man holding the pistol is recently shaved and wearing a brown frockcoat and boots. He looks too clean for a bushranger but too dirty for a man of property. Mr Kidney notes the scar on his throat and takes him to be a settler, a former military man, lately arrived in search of some affordable parcel of land. The man says nothing, but reaches up and gently relieves Mr Kidney of his fowling piece.

'I said I am rescued, sir, and God has made you the instrument.'

Robert Lefebure alias Quincy tosses the fowling piece into the bushes. 'I have no use for instruments,' he says.

'You misunderstand me,' says the chaplain, shifting in his saddle. 'You are the instrument by which I am delivered out of the wilderness. The instrument, sir...'

'I am no man's instrument.'

'You are the Almighty's,' Mr Kidney declares warmly.

Quincy laughs and hoiks a gob of spittle from the back of his throat.

'Pardon my effusiveness, sir. I did not mean to give offence. I was overcome by relief. Please, sir, you must accept my apology.' The chaplain gives an awkward smile. 'A party of marines treated me most barbarously and left me to my misfortune. I have been riding since dawn with nothing to eat or drink. If you had some rum, sir, or a little whisky or wine, I should be instantly revived.'

'What are you doing here?'

'What am I doing here?' Mr Kidney dabs at his face with a handkerchief. 'Why, sir, I am here because my horse brought me here. Of its own accord and without my consent.' He looks down magnanimously at the offending beast, which carries on tugging at the long grass. 'Believe me, had I not been waylaid, I should already be back in Hobart Town. There are many…anxious souls…waiting upon my return.'

'And why would they be anxious?'

'Because…' The chaplain stops himself. He senses something sinister in the stranger's question. He sits up straight. 'They worry, sir. One cannot stop one's friends from worrying.'

Quincy laughs again. 'You think you will be missed?'

'Indeed, sir. I am most certain of it.'

'There are many who think they will be missed yet no-one will come looking for them.'

'No doubt that is true. But I assure you, sir, not in my case.'

'Then you will not mind lending me your horse.'

'I beg your pardon?'

Rather than repeat himself, Quincy raises his pistol until it is pointing straight at the chaplain's nose.

Fear and outraged pride lift Mr Kidney several inches out of his saddle. 'Do you not know me, sir? I am Thomas Kidney, chaplain of this colony. I am the Lord's to command. I will not have a weapon pointed at me.'

'I won't say it again.'

The chaplain disentangles his boot heels from the stirrups and lowers himself solemnly to the ground. He drops to his knees. 'Surely, sir, you cannot intend to

desert me. I appeal to you, sir, as a Christian, Take me
with you. Don't leave me...'

~

The following is the Substance of a Letter delivered to this
Office at a quarter after 10 o'clock last Night by a
Gentleman who claimed to have received the same from
the Hand of Mr SALTER at the Crossroads near Bagdad:

'On Monday Afternoon, having lost all Trace of the
Person whose Tracks we had followed since Breakfast, we
crossed the Jordan River at Broad Marsh. Our Intention
was to reach Bagdad by Nightfall and resume our Search
after a sound Night's Sleep.

'Hardly had we sighted the River when Dr Banes
perceived a leather Waistcoat upon the Bridge, which
Garment, upon close Inspection, was found to have several
Blood Stains upon it. The Blood being, in the Opinion of
Dr Banes, freshly spilt, we resolved to expend a Quarter of
an Hour in Search of the Victim.

'This Period having passed, with no Clue to his
Whereabouts, we crossed the Bridge, and were approach-
ing the Village of Bagdad, when we discovered the
unfortunate Man, somewhat debauched by Drink, lying in
a Ditch. Mrs Fitzgerald at once named him as William
Dyer, the Father of the Seal Pup, or Sooterkin, whose safe
Recovery, together with that of the Boy, comprises the chief
Object of our Expedition.

'Dyer being, in his present State, in no Condition to
narrate the Particulars of his Experience, we were obliged
to convey him to Bagdad, and to procure a Quantity of Ale

and dry Tobacco, without which he would not consent to recount the Events that had befallen him. Those Comforts having been administered, and the greater Part of them consumed, he proceeded, amid prodigious Apologies to his Wife and Son and loud Appeals to his Conscience, to make the following Extraordinary Confession:

'That the Seal Baby, which he called Arthur, had been stolen by a Man named Quincy whom he had invited to his Home for the Purpose of meeting the Infant. And that he, the lawful Father, had conspired in the Theft, by which he hoped to gain an immediate Profit and build a Brick House with several Rooms, that he might be reckoned one of the grand Gentlemen of the Colony and his Wife a Lady, with a Brass Bed and Candlesticks. He alleged that Dr Banes had also made an Offer, of the most extravagant Kind, but that the Mother would not accept.

'Quincy, however, had tricked him and slipped away from the Settlement without Warning, with the Aim (he supposed) of selling the Infant in Secret, and keeping the Money for himself. He therefore determined to follow the Villain, and punish him, and but for some Delay at the Barley Mow in Black Snake would have overrun him in a Trice. (Dr Banes pronounced the Man an inveterate Liar and Drunkard.)

'Yesterday, while crossing the Bridge at Broad Marsh, he was set upon from behind and in the Course of a mortal Struggle was struck with a Pistol Butt and pushed into the River. Quincy, his Assailant, spewed Curses upon him, and accused him of Treachery, and said the Sailors would not take the Sooterkin and there was no Profit to be got from a Bastard. (This Remark the Father took to be a Slight on himself, and wept, whereupon we were obliged to comfort him with another Mug of Ale and more Tobacco.)

'Upon pulling himself from the River, Dyer found the Remnants of a Map, with diverse Marks and Crosses whose Meaning he could not tell, but which Mr Sculley at once identified as the Coast at Grindstone Bay.'

~

IT IS not Mr Kidney's intention to walk all night, but having started he finds he cannot stop. He walks on blindly, with no sense of time or place, pausing every so often to blow his nose, as if careful maintenance will allow him to sniff his way to Hobart Town.

The sky is huge and empty—a vast cathedral dome lit by a half moon. Mr Kidney gazes among the trees and wonders if Mrs Jakes has a cold fowl waiting for him. The leg of a goose, perhaps, with some of Mrs Jakes's burnt cumberland sauce. And a handful of cold potatoes. Some green beans. A small pot of mustard.

Somewhere ahead of him an owl hoots. He hears its wings flapping in the darkness. He stops again and fills his nostrils with the stink of stagnant water.

Mr Kidney's nose has led him to the edge of Bradley's Lagoon, a shallow pond choked with reeds and rushes. Above it rises a rocky spur that has saved numerous travellers lost in the endless shaggy forest. Were Mr Kidney to make the effort to climb it, he would find a marker directing him to the nearest farmhouse.

But the chaplain is unaware of his good fortune, or of any fortune at all, and wanders on, muttering to himself and scratching his backside in a way that suggests his breeches are full of ants.

He reprimands Mrs Jakes for having overdone the potatoes, turning them to flour despite his instructions to monitor their progress with a skewer. The goose itself is overcooked. There is not enough ginger in the cumberland sauce and she has forgotten the capers.

He passes close by the edge of the lagoon and, as if fed up with the inconvenience of wearing a coat, drops it among the reeds.

~

The Prisoners MICHAEL BRODIE, DANIEL SEPTON and JAMES WATTS, whose Escapades have often been reported in our Columns, committed a Robbery at Clarence Plains on Monday Evening; after which they became so excessively intoxicated by Spirits (a Part of their Plunder) as to quarrel amongst Themselves. The Fury of their Disputation was such as to cause the Men to draw their Weapons, and thereupon to discharge them, as a Consequence of which SEPTON and WATTS were killed outright and BRODIE mortally wounded. The Corpses of all three being recovered the following Day, together with the Entirety of their Plunder, at no Expense to the public Purse, and little Inconvenience to the Magistrate, we are enjoined to propose the prompt Distribution of such Liquor and Firearms as will swiftly rid the Colony of their Companions.

~

The following Letter was delivered to the Printer at a quarter before five this Tuesday Afternoon by a Boy who was given it by Mr SALTER, with the most solemn Instruction to deliver it without Delay:

'The drunken Wretch, who proclaimed himself Father to the Sooterkin, did not choose to submit his Story to further Examination in the Morning, but stole away during the Night, having helped himself to several Bottles of Mr Sculley's private Tonics, under the Delusion that they were Liquor. The Chart, by which we had intended to steer our Course, was likewise gone, and no amount of Hunting could discover either Man or Map.

'Our hopes of Success therefore rested on the Shoulders of Mr Sculley, whose Recollection of the Map, together with some few Marks he had inscribed in a Notebook, were now our only Guide in the Matter. We floundered blind until Lunchtime, when we were fortunate to come upon a Trader's Cart, with some Morsels that proved more than adequate to our Needs, and fortified us for the Adventure that lay ahead.

'Hardly had we finished eating when Mr Sculley sighted the very Thing we had been looking for, namely the Bluff known as Bradley's Lookout, which until that Point had been obscured by the Trees. A Track being nearby, and the coastal Road less than a Mile distant, we committed ourselves at a Gallop, or such Approximation of it as we could manage in our exhausted State, and commenced the Pursuit which, we hoped, would lead to the Rescue of the Sooterkin, the Capture of the Father, and the Release of the Boy.

'Alas, Mr Sculley being somewhat weakened by the Loss of his Tonics, and the rest of us untutored in the Art of Tracking, we could but guess at the Meaning of the fresh Spoor and Imprints that conspired to lead us back into the Woods from which we had recently emerged, and were many Times obliged to separate in Order to establish the correct Path. This, however, we have now done and, but for the Time expended in composing this Narrative, we would doubtless have run our Quarry to Ground.

'We have found a Shepherd's Hut, with some Signs of recent Occupation, and were perplexed in the Extreme by the Discovery of a leather Satchel containing a Hymnal, the property of the Revd Mr Kidney. It is Mr Sculley's Conviction that we are near the Coast, and we expect at any Minute to be rewarded with a Sight of the Ocean. Thus, having found a willing Volunteer to deliver this Missive, we set off again with the warmest Hopes of Success in our Quest.'

~

THE WIDOW'S horse is only a small chestnut mare but it runs like a thoroughbred. Before long she and Ned are over the hills and cantering through a valley beside a fast brown river.

The cart is an irregular shape, a sort of rhombus on wheels, which Mrs Slade says was built by a carpenter down on his luck and is not much to look at but could carry a ton of potatoes if she had them. She and Ned are squashed together on a plank that quivers when they go over a pothole and makes the old woman's teeth chatter.

They are following a track which was laid out by the deputy surveyor with a chain and bullock cart and is the only road for miles that didn't disappear in the floods. Ned wants to know how she can be sure it is the right road. The old woman points to a pile of fresh droppings. 'Trust me, Ned. He was here before us.'

The hills fall away on one side of the valley and the track turns back on itself. In the distance is a rocky outcrop which the old woman calls a bluff, and below the bluff is a lagoon half suffocated with reeds. 'That is Bradley's Lagoon,' she says with a chuckle, 'and that is Bradley's Bluff above it, and Bradley's Lookout nearby and I dare say the grass is Bradley's and all the trees and if a horse shits on the road it is Bradley's turd and he's welcome to it.'

She cackles away as the cart slithers through the mud. The widow's old carcass rattles like a bag of bones and Ned wonders again if she is some kind of witch or termagant who can read the future with entrails and track a man by his smell. If there is such a thing as intyvishun, which a person can use to find out what they don't know already, then Mrs Slade, he thinks, must have it in spades.

Ned asks where the road is heading. She looks at him for a while and says, 'I haven't been down it in a dozen years, boy, but I believe it will take us to the sea at Oyster Bay or Grindstone Bay or somewhere in between.' She glances at him out of the corner of her eye and gives a little twitch on the reins. 'Tell me, Ned, have you got no brothers?'

'Only Arthur, ma'am.'

'What about sisters?'

'I had two sisters but they died and was buried in the graveyard and Mam says it was the weeping that set a pup growing inside her but Pa told me once it was scallops.'

Mrs Slade tosses a potato out of her skirts and says, 'I believe it, Ned.'

Ned looks down at the track rushing beneath them. He cannot believe it was weeping that did it, or else women would always be giving birth to pups and rabbits and kittens. But nor can he believe it was scallops, as he has seen many convict women eating scallops that had boys just like him, or girls, and if scallops were enough to start a pup growing inside you, what about crayfish and salt beef?

They ride for two hours with the morning sun in their eyes before the trees change and the air turns suddenly cool. They pass a gorge with vines and tree ferns and a waterfall tumbling over rocks and Ned asks Mrs Slade if she heard the devils howling last night.

'That wasn't devils,' she says.

'What was it?'

'That was blacks calling to each other. You will make a poor shepherd, Ned, if you cannot tell one from the other.' She lets the horse trot for a while. 'Mind you,' she adds, 'they're both sheep killers.'

The sun is glittering in the canopy and the potatoes have settled and Ned is starting to feel sleepy when the widow pulls up and shakes him awake. 'Look at that,' she says, pointing at a piece of paper lying under a bush. She tells him to hop down and fetch it. It's a blank page from a prayer book or a Bible or somesuch. There's a neat hole in it, as if someone skewered it with a stick. There are more horse droppings nearby ('but not so fresh as the last,' Mrs Slade remarks sagely) and a muddle of hoofprints. The old woman stares at the paper and holds it up to the sun so that

it is as translucent as her own skin. Then she slips it into
the pocket of her apron and says, 'He's not the one we're
after, Ned.'

They press on. Now Ned is wide awake, scouring the
woods for a glimpse of the gentleman who dropped the
paper.

After a while they come across a battered prayer book
and then a silver brandy flask trodden into the mud. Mrs
Slade shakes her head and says the man who dropped them
has lost his wits, like her own husband who went out one
morning and never came back, and others who go walking into rivers, or blow their brains out because of the voices
in their heads. If it's not voices, she says, it's the woods or
the birds or the blacks hooting in the dark or the silence
that drives them mad.

Ned listens and says, 'Is it true that flogging can turn a
man out of his wits?'

'Who told you that?' she asks.

Ned cannot give a name as the idea is his own.

The old woman rolls the question around in her head
before answering. 'It may be true, Ned,' she says, 'but I
never saw it happen and I believe it is them that order the
floggings that are maddest, and them that receive them are
no madder than the rest of us.' She reaches over and
grips his elbow. 'But if a person can lose their wits through
loneliness, Ned, this is the place.'

She sends him down to pick up the flask and the prayer
book. 'I never heard of a woman blowing her brains out,'
she says jauntily. 'A woman's got too much sense.'

Her voice stops.

She raises her left hand and points at a figure beside the

road: a man, stripped to his stockings, bent against a tree. Ned can't tell whether he is squatting or kneeling, whether they have caught him in his prayers or his defecations. The widow slows the cart until they are hardly moving. Even the mare is bemused, pricking its ears and shaking its head from side to side.

He is a fat bald man with black whiskers and a fleece of black hair down his spine, like the bristles on a boar. His waistcoat and breeches are lying nearby and he has thrown his boots off. His shirt is impaled on a bush. The sun has turned him as pink as a side of bacon.

They are almost upon him when he turns his head. His mouth opens but no sound comes out. It's Mr Kidney, all wild-eyed and bedraggled, with cracked lips and bruises and vines clinging to his whiskers. He's shaking all over. There are tears rolling down his cheeks. He stares at them one after the other—Ned, the widow and her horse—and hangs his head.

Mrs Slade reaches across, afraid that Ned might leap out, although Ned is sitting as if paralysed, his mouth open and his hands gripping the wooden bench. 'Is it the chaplain?' she asks. He nods.

Mr Kidney struggles to his feet. He stands before them as naked as a puppy, but for the stockings on his feet and a chain around his neck with a silver cross on it. The old woman doesn't turn away but gazes at his prick, which is poking up at the sky (or at heaven, as she says later) and garlanded with leaves. The chaplain waddles towards them with his arms open. He falls with a great sigh upon the mare's neck and cries, 'You have brought the goose!'

Mrs Slade waits a long time before answering, 'We have, sir.' She hands him a wineskin filled with water, which he puts to his broken lips and gulps like a mug of the finest claret. The widow whispers at Ned to climb over and make room for Mr Kidney among the potatoes. They have no blankets but there is a folded tarpaulin in the corner.

Mrs Slade clambers down and fetches the chaplain's breeches and asks softly if he would consent to stepping into them and if it would suit him better to wear boots and if he would oblige her by putting on his shirt, as the sun is high and he will burn without it. Mr Kidney smiles and does what he is told and says he will be ready for the goose in a short while. 'Pray be careful,' he mumbles, 'that the cumberland sauce is not burnt.' The widow brushes the leaves out of his whiskers and uses the corner of her apron to wipe the mud off his cheeks.

'Hop down, Ned,' she says quietly. 'We must not keep Mr Kidney waiting.'

The chaplain is too tired to climb aboard but they push and heave and shoulder him until he is folded like a parcel in the widow's tarpaulin. He looks around and smiles, as if surprised to find himself in such salubrious surroundings, then lowers his head on a piece of sacking and falls asleep.

Some miles further on, a track joins the road at a bend. There is no stone or post to say where it has come from, but there are fresh hoofprints in the mud and a pair of crisp new furrows. 'A dog cart has been here before us,' says the widow. Mr Kidney whimpers and rolls over on his side.

They are soon out of the woods but the sun is dropping and the widow's chestnut mare is not pulling as hard as she was. The country is hilly on both sides and there is a steely glow in the sky. The widow says it is the sea's reflection and will guide them as it gets dark.

Parts of the land have been fenced off and cleared, with some of the stumps pulled out and the rest left to rot in the ground. There's a wheat stack standing by itself in the middle of a field, and a poor excuse for a shelter, and the beginnings of a stockyard. Cattle look up from their chewing and stare at the cart as it trundles by.

The labourers who made the road have done a careless job. Time and again the wooden wheels batter against stumps that nobody could be bothered to dig out. The horse is tired and stumbles in the mud and as they go over a hump the chaplain slides out of his tarpaulin like a calf being born.

The dark is coming down fast around their ears. The road turns, then swings back again and begins to drop steeply towards the sea. The chestnut mare sniffs the salt and picks up her pace as Ned struggles to get the chaplain back into his tarpaulin. Mr Kidney seems perfectly at ease. His hands are folded on his belly like someone dozing in a hammock. As they clatter down the hill Ned wonders if he will ever wake up.

The thunder of the waves rushes up to meet them. Ned feels his heart pounding inside his ribs. Mr Kidney grunts and rolls over and the potatoes rearrange themselves around him.

The chestnut mare is sweating and straining. It's as much as Mrs Slade can do to keep the animal from leaving the road and careering down to the sea. The widow has her head down and her teeth clenched and Ned thinks that any minute now they will be smashed against a tree and killed.

Then all of a sudden the road veers right and they are in a hollow, with a great sand dune ahead of them and some ragged cliffs looming beyond. Mrs Slade tugs hard on the reins and the mare pulls up in an instant, as if there were anchors in her shoes. The widow catches him gaping and gives a short laugh, then skips down into the sand, leaving the chaplain asleep in his tarpaulin.

Behind the dune they can hear the surf crashing on the beach and the whistle of the sea sucking it back. The air has a crisp salty smell, not like the rank seaweed stink of the harbour.

A white moon is peeping out between the clouds. The widow scolds Ned for not bringing a lantern (she never mentioned it until now) and says they will be lucky to see their own faces in half an hour.

If there were ever any tracks or footprints in the sand, the wind has blown them away. Ned and the old woman clamber up the back of the dune and crouch among the saltbushes. The beach stretches away to the left. On the other side are low black cliffs crowned with mops of long grass. There is a shelf jutting into the sea and some jagged rocks scattered about. Every ledge on the cliff face is crowded with shrieking gulls.

The old woman says she has heard of sealers rowing out to the shelf when the seals are gathered there and killing a hundred before breakfast. She grips Ned's sleeve. 'If the seal pup or sooterkin or whatever you are pleased to call it…' Her voice peters out and she pinches his cheek with her gaunt fingers. 'Come, Ned,' she hisses. 'We must get closer.'

They slide down the face of a dune and wade through

the soft sand, Mrs Slade in front and Ned scuttling behind. He wants to know what it was she was going to say but he's afraid to hear the answer. He never imagined until now that Arthur could be mistaken for a common seal, that the pup could end up clubbed and skinned like those in the harbour.

'Sshhh,' says Mrs Slade, although Ned has not opened his mouth. She points to a dark shape at the water's edge. 'What is it, Ned?' she whispers. 'Is it moving?'

Ned creeps ahead and peers into the gloom. The sky is a deep blue-black but the surf is glittering in the moonlight. 'A horse,' he says.

'Is it a black horse?' she asks, cocking the musket.

Ned whispers that it is not a black horse but Mr Kidney's piebald. Mrs Slade frowns and rubs her eyes. Her skin looks waxy, like the tailings of a candle left in a dish. With the moon behind her, Ned can almost see right through her. She is like a skeleton with skin on it.

They hear voices in the distance and see gulls swooping from the cliffs.

'How many are there, Ned?'

Ned can make out indistinct shapes moving in the darkness, two figures a long way off who appear to be quarrelling, a dog cart bogged in the sand and several figures huddled around a flickering lantern.

They reach a gap in the dunes where a rivulet snakes out of a shallow ravine. Ned hesitates, as if expecting the widow to shirk the challenge of crossing it. 'Tsk, boy,' she hisses, 'I am not a corpse. It is forty years since I have skipped a stream but I dare say I've not lost the knack.' She hitches up her skirts and splashes across without waiting for him.

As they move closer to the figures they watch seagulls

tumbling from their ledges and wheeling across the moon-lit sky in a great shimmering arc.

Ned and Mrs Slade reach the dog cart, which has been abandoned by its occupants and is buried up to its axles in the sand. There are now half a dozen figures shouting and squabbling over the lantern.

'Who are they, Ned?'

Ned recognises a tall sharp-faced man clutching a bundle to his chest. 'It's him,' he cries.

'Who else?'

'Sculley the bodysnatcher is there, and a lady. I think it's the schoolmarm. I can't tell the others.'

The little man in the black frockcoat—Mr Sculley—is holding something in his hand: perhaps a purse. Quincy crouches down on the sand and begins unwrapping the object. Mr Sculley says something. Quincy shakes his head. Mr Sculley takes a step closer. He takes the spectacles off his nose and rubs them with his handkerchief as Quincy reaches inside the bundle of rags and pulls out the seal pup by the scruff of its neck.

At that instant a man emerges from the dunes behind them. It's William Dyer, with a bottle of Mr Sculley's tonic in one hand, and an axe in the other, roaring at them to leave the sooterkin alone or be cut into pieces.

'Who is it, Ned?' cries Mrs Slade, pulling the boy back by his red neckerchief. 'Do you know him?'

Ned breaks free of the old woman's grasp and starts running. 'Pa! Pa!' he screams. 'They've got Arthur!'

As Dyer reels towards them, waving the axe above his head, Mr Kidney's piebald gelding takes fright and gallops across the beach. Quincy hesitates for a second, and in that second Dr Banes tries to snatch the seal pup. While trying to decide whose skull to cleave first, William Dyer trips and falls face down in the sand. The axe flies through the air, narrowly missing Banes but taking a sizeable piece out of his hat.

With Dyer spreadeagled on the sand, and Banes trembling with shock, the pup darts between Mr Sculley's legs. Suddenly it catches Ned's scent in the wind and barks with delight. Quincy drops to his knees and tries to smother it, but the pup rolls over and starts wriggling towards the sea.

A seagull swoops out of the darkness, then another, then a hundred more, all squealing and scratching and tearing at the tatty brown coat as Quincy crawls after the pup on his hands and knees.

Voices cry out in the darkness.

'Catch the sooterkin!'

'Don't let the creature escape!'

The pup pauses for a moment as the sea rushes to meet it. Ned shouts, 'Don't stop, Arthur!' As Quincy flails at the seagulls, Ned sees the seal pup nuzzle the waves. It lets out a joyous yelp as the water closes around it and the undertow sweeps it away. Ned watches its smooth round head rise out of the surf before the pup slides under for the last time and is gone. Ignoring his father's drunken groans, Ned wades in up to his waist and stands for a long time staring out to sea until Mrs Slade goes to fetch him back.

~

It affords us the greatest Satisfaction to report the safe Return of Mr KIDNEY, whose Absence, though brief, caused such Agitation among his Admirers. Our Enthusiasm is tempered, however, by the Sight of that eloquent Gentleman reduced to tremulous Silence by the Severity of his Adventures. We are assured by no lesser Personage than Mrs SWEETWATER that he wants for Nothing in the Affections of his Wellwishers, among whom she appears to be Foremost. We are inclined to hope that, though his Mind has wandered, it may be restored to us by the Healing Influence of Time and the Sober Attentions of his Housekeeper. Until then our Curiosity must be satisfied by the Memoirs of a Boy, EDWARD DYER, whose Perseverance is entirely to thank for his Rescue, and whose astonishing Narrative, with many remarkable Digressions and mature Observations, will be published in a Special Supplement, signed by the Boy in his own Hand, at the Cost of a Shilling.

~

YOU ARE still here, moist-eyed from excitement, or relief, or both. Summer has arrived and Hobart Town is baking in the sun. The Customs House is full of sweating clerks and splitting furniture. The rivulet stinks like a cesspool and horses are going mad from the dust. The meat store is humming with blowflies and the salt beef is ready to walk again.

Ned can't forget the pup and hears a familiar bark one night while hunting for scallops on the rocks under the chaplain's jetty. A luminous mass of seaweed is lapping against the pillars. As Ned searches the waves a furry head appears. The creature swims about for a minute before slipping away, then pops up again and hangs for a moment stroking its whiskers and seeming to smile. Ned calls and whistles and claps his hands. Then a wave breaks over the seaweed and when the froth clears the apparition has vanished, leaving a pair of sailors' pants rolling in the swell, the pockets stuffed with mussels. Which, says his mother, tossing a knob of fat in the skillet, is a handsome trick in anyone's book.

~

We are this Morning favoured with the surprising News that the Mother of the SEAL PUP is again with Child, a bare FIVE MONTHS after the Delivery of that illustrious Infant whose singular Gifts inspired such earnest Reflection among those disposed to contemplate them. Prudence alone prevents us from speculating on the Shape of the Lady's Expectations and the Manner by which that felicitous Offspring was conceived. Suffice it to say that such remarkable Fertility, wrenched from the Barrenness of Sorrow, must instil great Hopes for the Survival and Prosperity of this beleaguered Colony.